STRANGE CHOICES

НЕОБИЧАЙНИ РЕШЕНИЯ

A Voyeuristic Peek into The Lives of
People Around You

BARI BAZILI

Author:Barı Bazili

Original Cover Art: Adam J Ferguson
Cover Design: KISMET Publishers Ltd

Editor- English- Denver Murphy
Editor- Bulgarian- Radostina Goranova/ Радостина Горанова

KISMET Publishers Ltd
71-75, Shelton Street, Covent Garden, London, WC2H 9JQ
Publisher@kismetpublishers.co.uk
www.KismetPublishers.co.uk

Note From The Publisher

November 1968, Sly and the Family Stone's "Everyday People"

I am everyday people, yeah, yeah

There is a blue one who can't accept
The green one for living with
A fat one tryin' to be a skinny one

New author, seasoned podcaster and journalist Bari Bazili brings her stories a blend of seemingly ordinary everyday people who in an effort just to be themselves and comfortable in their own skin end up making strange decisions that they have to live with and sometimes die with. A voyeuristic peek into the lives of the people you encounter everyday.

When I met Bari I was immediately drawn to a woman who was different from me, yet the same as me. She grew up under the reign of communism. I grew where democracy and capitalism ruled. She was writing reviews and translating Turkish series into English and her native tongue Bulgarian as a hobby. She had such a way with words I thought surely she must be an author. She could text something that had me howling with laughter out loud.

This is not the nature of these stories; perhaps she will grace us with those stories in a second book.

For now delve into the world according to Bari Bazili. Experience what is going on in the minds, hearts and souls of everyday people

Ramona Harper Ferguson
KISMET Publishers Ltd
The Conversation Starters
READ MORE. CONNECT MORE. CARE MORE

For more information on other authors or to sign up for the KISMET Newsletter Conversation Starters
kismetpublishers.com

"a big enormous thanks to

... my husband and my sons who have always made me feel special, safe and surprised.

... Ramona Harper who believed in me more than I believed in myself.

... Adam Ferguson who is the most patient and enduring project manager in the world.

... Engin Akyürek who is not just a damn good actor but also a story teller who inspires story telling; and a human who inspires the best in humanity.

And to all strangers in my life who provoked me to dip into their lives...

Table Of Content

Note From The Publisher iii

How To Become a Writer 9

Shopping 19

Fear 29

Hitchhiking 37

Assembling 49

Traffic Jam 65

Strange Choice 77

To Be Continued... 97

Binoculars 103

КАК СЕ СТАВА ПИСАТЕЛ 117

ШОПИНГ 129

СТРАХ 139

СТОПАДЖИЙКАТА 145

СГЛОБЯВАНЕ 157

ЗАДРЪСТВАНЕ.................................171

НЕОБИКНОВЕНО РЕШЕНИЕ 181

ПРОДЪЛЖЕНИЕ 199

БИНОКЪЛ 207

ТЕРАПИЯ ЗА СЪРЦЕ 217

How To Become a Writer

Elena was a long-awaited child. Her mother gave birth to her aged 42. But she was born with a defect – her right foot was turned ninety degrees to the left. In the distant years of communism, operations abroad were not even a thing. The Bulgarian doctors said there was no point in operating on her. She was prescribed special orthopedic shoes.

At school she was made fun of, she was exempted from physical education. She never went to a party, no one ever asked her to a dance. Although she walked without crutches, her gait was ugly, swaying left and right, slow and sluggish.

On top of all, in eighth grade she found out that she would have to wear glasses. The ugly plastic frames hid the only thing she relied on to make people like her – her beautiful face.

STRANGE CHOICES

She loved to read, read a lot and even wrote. Her high school literature teacher praised her constantly, gave her A's, predicted her future as a literature expert, read excerpts from her essays to the others. But in the hormone-dominated age of high school, literary ability was more the cause of further ridicule than admiration.

She dreamed of studying literature, but was afraid that if she would become a teacher, she would not have the strength to face her students one day. She imagined that the taunts would pick up where they had left off in school. She imagined herself limping from the door to her desk when walking into class, and giggling is heard from the side.

Still, she decided to apply for the university. The day before the entrance exam, her mother died. Then Elena had to start work. The best offer she had was to sell newspapers in a newsstand at the intersection of two major boulevards in Plovdiv[1].

Then communism fell. Her father also passed away. She was left alone in the small apartment. And in the newsstand. Several parliaments and governments came one after another, Bulgaria became a European country, Ladas[2] and Trabants[3] disappeared from the boulevards on her both sides, Toyotas and Mercedes

---

[1] Plovdiv – the second biggest city in Bulgria
[2] Lada – a Soviet car
[3] Trabant – an Eastern Germany car

replaced them. The newsstand itself was bought by one businessman, then by another, then by a third. The stand itself was replaced by a bigger one, then by a smaller one, then by a yellow one. At one time, they repaired the sidewalk on which it was placed, during which Elena went on forced leave. Then they planted trees around, then the trees grew tall and began to shade the newsstand. Then people almost stopped buying newspapers.

Her working hours never changed – at seven in the morning she unlocked the newsstand, took out the newspapers and magazines, and arranged them on the wide shelf. When it rained, she covered them with plastic. At half past seven, the distributor came and dropped off the new issues. She had a miniature stool, a large canvas purse for the change, a tiny battery-operated fan to save her in the summer heat, and a thick woolen scarf from her grandmother, which she kept under the shelf inside and used in winter to wrap her legs and feet. At three o'clock in the afternoon she put the papers back in, locked up, and went home. Every day except Sunday.

Each new owner of the newsstand didn't fire her because they felt sorry for her, because she worked conscientiously, and because she was content with a small salary.

At half past three, Elena went to the supermarket, bought strictly specified things on strictly specified days, went home, cooked dinner for herself, and wrote. She read and wrote. Until midnight. Then she fell asleep and at six in the morning the cycle went on.

Every year they made a new pair of orthopedic custom shoes for her because they wore out quickly. At home she walked in slippers with special footbeds. She bought clothes four times a year, from the same stores. Over the years, some stores disappeared, new ones appeared, and she felt stressed every time she had to find a new store.

She had no friends. She only knew the people from her dwelling house, and that was because they knew her mother and father. But the elderly families passed away one by one and the apartments were bought by other people. Elena did not know them. The only ones who could tell who she was were the orthopedists and orthopedic shoe makers. To everyone else, she was a limping middle-aged woman. No one knew what her feelings were, or even if she had any feelings at all.

And she herself wondered, too. She was friendly with the newsstand customers, she knew almost everyone by face, some of them even by name. The more talkative ones shared thing or two from their lives with her.

There was a tall, wiry old man who wore a cap both in winter and summer, lived in the next intersection, and his old lady had died. He was a former engineer, with two children living abroad. He took care of his household all alone, he didn't miss buying a newspaper every morning. He felt nostalgia for communism.

There were two old women who had nothing in common with each other, but looked so alike that Elena sometimes confused them. Both bought children's books for their granddaughters when they came to visit. Little books with coloring pictures. Then their granddaughters grew up, but the two women kept coming to buy crossword puzzles.

There was a Miss Sudoku – a spiffy intellectual aunty who kept track of when the most difficult Sudoku puzzles would come, and bought only them. She didn't even ask about the price.

There were Gypsies who asked her if she had any old newspapers for free. But Elena had to account to the owner for the old newspapers, too, and so she didn't give them any.

She knew by the newspapers who voted for which party, who had taken their monthly pension, who was fascinated by the supernatural issues.

At the dawn of the democratic times, she even had to sell erotic newspapers. She was horribly ashamed and hid them under the other papers but the owner of the newsstand was angry at her for decreasing their sales as a consequence. She didn't dare look into the eyes of those who bought them. Thank God, they later banned the outdoor sale of such papers and she breathed a sigh of relief.

December usually started the sale of calendars for the following year, and then the trade turned livelier. At some point she was also selling greeting cards, but no one bought greeting cards anymore.

There were no young customers.

With some she exchanged two or three words; others just handed over the money, took their newspapers and left without even looking at her.

She used to take a holiday once a year for one week. But she wondered what to do in these days. She usually slept late. She never left Plovdiv.

✱✱✱

Everything Elena accumulated in her head and heart, she poured out on sheets of paper. When she started, she was writing by hand. There were hundreds of notebooks written from cover to cover, packed into croissant boxes. Later she decided to buy a computer for herself. She just walked into a computer store and said she wanted a computer. The young boy in the store asked her what kind of a computer she was looking for, and she remained silent.

"What will you use it for?"

"For writing."

Her first laptop and her first connection to Internet were the most exciting things of her entire life. She started going to bed later and later because she began also reading on the Internet. She kept everything she wrote in neatly arranged folders in her laptop. Short stories, essays, short novels, even two full-length novels.

When she realized she wouldn't be able to study at the university, she began to visit the National Library and systematically read textbooks on literature. She used to sit on her little stool in the newsstand (or next to it if it was too hot), to read diligently and take notes. Then she used to look at the people who passed on the sidewalk; the drivers in the cars that stopped at the crosswalk; her customers, who were slowly but inexorably replaced by other customers over the years, and then she described them.

A short teenage girl on a scooter passed slowly, her nose stuck in the phone, with a lollipop in her mouth, which she absentmindedly pulled out and waved in step with the invisible music in her headphones... That evening she turned into a secret agent, giving coded signals to her colleagues by waving a lollipop in the air...

A smug, fat driver of an expensive BMW, whizzing through the crosswalk without stopping, in the evening turned into a baleful hippopotamus in a fable...

A stooped old woman with teary eyes, clutching a cup of yogurt, turned into a fairy-godmother who tests people's kindness...

A merry company of tipsy American tourists in patterned shirts rescued a three-legged dog and smuggled it onto the plane...

Children with schoolbags on their backs were substituted for quarreling neighbors...

Bums begging for money for cigarettes turned into undercover tax-inspectors...

The small, dark apartment with ugly communist furniture used to fill up with people, images, voices, and events. Elena was so exhausted imagining and describing their life that she had no energy left for the life outside. She walked, indifferent and hipped on her daily route to the newsstand, then to the supermarket; said "good morning" to the customers in an even voice, moved her stool in the heat of the day according to the shade of the trees, and rarely felt hungry.

Everyone thought she was an unsociable and dry woman, devoid of intelligence and imagination.

She had no relatives but some distant paternal cousins. She had last seen them at her father's funeral. She didn't miss them now. She had her heroes, her passers-by on the boulevards, her city noises, buses, and swallows. She talked mostly to herself and her characters. She was careful not to do it while at work so people wouldn't think her crazy. But when she came home in the evening, she started talking – to herself; to the characters in the books she had read during the day; to the characters in the stories she was currently writing. She spoke out her entire number of words for the day in two hours, and then she was silent again. And she wrote. She wrote a diary of the day as it should have been.

She experienced the whole of world history sitting on her stool in or next to the newsstand – the fall of communism, the hyperinflation, 9/11, Bulgaria in the European Union, six governments, the COVID epidemic, the Ukrainian war... she read newspapers, watched the news, but what really interested her was how this ugly world could migrate into her stories, obey her imagination, and become what she wanted it to be. She never left Plovdiv. But she traveled the whole world on the Internet, on television, and in books. And she described it as she saw it.

***

One day she started coughing. And she didn't stop for four months. First she thought it was a flu, then COVID, then she realized it was something else. Thirty years of inhaling car fumes at one of the busiest intersections in the city had borne fruit – lung cancer. She, who had never smoked a single cigarette in her life, had lung cancer. Of both lungs. With many distractions.

She kept writing until the very end, even with the breathing mask on her face in the hospital. By then, she had returned to writing by hand. The nurses looked at her sympathetically, because the scribbles in her notebook were illegible. But they knew this calmed her down and helped her endure the pain.

There was not a single person at her funeral. The municipality buried her. The next day, the distant cousins put the apartment up for sale without even showing up. The buyer found boxes of notebooks and thought the previous owner had been a teacher. Out of curiosity, he started reading one of them.

***

And he became a famous writer. He published more than twenty books, some of which were translated abroad, and a film based on two of them was made. He gave extensive interviews in which he explained how his training in psychology helped him see the world through women's eyes. They called him "amazing" and "the first man who understood women".

Elena continued to live in her dragons, spies, teachers, waiters, beaches, policemen, hippos, and fairies. Albeit under a different name.

Shopping

It was all because of her. The stupid old cow. Puffed up and self-important, spiteful down to the very last cell of her pea brain. She sent him to do a makeup exam, and failed his graduation.

If he only had a father…

If only he had, but he hadn't. And that's why she took revenge on him with impunity. Simon's father defended his son, everyone in the school saw how he was leaning over Mrs. Tatcheva at the end of the school corridor, how he spoke to her quietly with clenched fists. And Simon graduated. But Boris had to do a makeup exam. She was looking at him with pursed lips and vengeful eyes, "I'm sorry, Boris. I warned you last year that if you keep going like this, you won't graduate." Then she slowly wrote a beautifully crafted number two.[4]

Well, he was not a luminary of literature. But she could have given him at least a three. But no, she had to take revenge on someone for the way Simon's father had humiliated her.

Then Boris had to find a job. How can one find a job in a fifteen-thousand-people-town? A town where your mother is one of five hairdressers – the most experienced but also the most elderly? She only makes enough money to pay their electricity and bills, and she has to go to Sofia[5] to buy her clothes from second-hand shops, so that her customers won't find out.

He conducted some research, asked questions here and there... he had to decide – either they move to live in Sofia, or he would go abroad. His mother resolutely refused to relocate, "I can't start from the beginning again, and look for new customers. Not in Sofia. I won't get used to the dirt and the noise. I'll get sick."

He began scanning the job ads abroad.

***

It was his first time on a plane, he was careful not to give himself away. He was ashamed that he hadn't been on one before now. He carefully watched his neighbor fasten his seatbelt, then without

---

[4] In the Bulgarian school grading system, the lowest grade is two, and the best grade is six.
[5] Sofia is the capital city of Bulgaria, about 1,5 million people city.

hesitation, felt his own and buckled it for the first time. He leaned back contentedly and looked out the window.

The pilot announced that they were starting to descend over Amsterdam, he felt vibrations and a slight discomfort in his stomach. My God, what a huge and shining city! Amsterdam was no bigger than Sofia, but it seemed to him a hundred times brighter. And the airport... the whole Sofia airport could fit into one gate of Amsterdam's. A wave of a completely foreign language washed over him and he felt panic. His English was mediocre, he could only understand ordinary things. Thank God, people were nice and sympathetic.

***

Second week...

In the second week he walked several kilometers a day around the company's endless warehouses. The only thing he managed to remember in Dutch was "goede dag" and "faarvel"[6]. He started work at seven in the morning, and ended at seven in the evening. He worked overtime of his own free will; there was nothing to do in the evening, anyway. Most of his colleagues were Poles and Romanians, he was the only Bulgarian. The town was small, at six in the evening the streets were deserted. He started learning Dutch

---

[6] *Goede dag* – Good afternoon (Dutch); *Faarvel* – Good bye (Dutch)

on the Internet, but in the evening he was tired, so he didn't make much progress.

His job was to roam around the warehouses and take down goods with corresponding codes from the shelves. The company was large, an international Internet-trading company probably run by Chinese, because almost all of their goods were Chinese… People from all over the world shopped online and had their orders packed here. He was the one who made sure that the order number and the item number matched. If there were any claims for wrongly shipped goods, the bosses recouped the reshipment costs from the workers' wages. So, he had to be damn careful.

He felt dizzy when he realized how many people shopped online. Everything from anti-fungal ointment to electric lawnmowers; from swimsuits to gas guns. Sometimes, besides checking the order numbers, he also glanced at the addresses. All of Europe, the Arab countries, Russia, North Africa, South America, the United States... well, literally the whole world!

He got excited when he saw a Bulgarian name and address for the first time.

Some man from Aytos[7] had ordered orchid seeds. Boris smiled. He felt good that what he personally would take off the shelf and

---

[7]Aytos – a town located in eastern Bulgaria, some 30 kilometers from the Bulgarian Black Sea cost

put in the gray plastic bag, would arrive in two days in Aytos, and some unknown Atanas would plant the seeds in pots, and wait for them to sprout.

He got into the habit of checking the addresses and paying special attention to the Bulgarian ones. There were not many. Bulgarians mainly bought clothes, cosmetics, various kitchen gadgets. Most of them were women. He liked to imagine what these people looked like, or their houses, or their families. Sometimes he looked at what they ordered and formed an opinion about their financial conditions, their tastes, their way of life. It was a kind of a change in the monotonous everyday life – all day work, then some cleaning and cooking, and then Internet on the phone. He didn't watch TV, he didn't understand anything anyway. He didn't communicate with his roommates – most of them drank a lot and loved fighting. And he wanted to stay away from trouble.

Sometimes when he was suffocated by nostalgia he talked to his mother, getting upset when he felt that she could hardly keep from crying. He dreamed of sitting in his favorite chair in the cafe behind the bus station, with the cheerful aunt Peppa bringing him coffee, telling him the gossip of the town, and complaining about her illnesses and her daughter – all within thirty seconds. He couldn't stand the Dutch tomatoes and washy soups. He wanted real food. A quiet fury bubbled up in his chest every time he thought of the stupid cow Mrs. Tatcheva. He was here because of her! Because of her nasty little mean soul! He fantasized about making enough money to pay two stocky guys to beat her up, and she would never know where this had come from.

It was a normal Friday, such things didn't happen on Friday. On Fridays, everything was fast because the days off were coming – no one was moseying along as they didn't want to risk getting extra work for the weekend. But it happened! He saw the inscription "Bulgaria" on the envelope, and out of habit he read the name and address. He blinked twice, then he turned the envelope to the light and read it again. *"Svetoslava Tatcheva, 29 Archangel Michael Street..."* And his town! He sat down on the cart, feeling a sudden need to drink some water. The stupid cow was shopping on the Internet! He had never imagined it. An address from his town had never appeared thus far. Everything in this town was so slow, so sleepy and frozen that sometimes it seemed to him that there was no Internet there at all.

And the mean old Tatcheva rummaging through websites and shopping with a card... it was a sci-fi.

But the name and address was written clearly. He read the order, looked at the number... it was for a dress. A formal tasteless cheap synthetic Chinese dress. For twenty-three Euros and thirty-five cents. Double discount. She must have been invited to a wedding and decided to show off. Who knew the lies she would tell about buying it from Sofia, from some boutique. Malice flooded him like never before. That stupid and ugly dress he was holding in his hands, wrapped in rough nylon, was going to stretch over her disgusting ass and her sagging fat arms. He wanted to enchant the dress so that when she put it on, it would suddenly burst into flames and burn her alive. It was impossible for him not fulfill the order. Well, he could put in a dress three sizes smaller, but that would only slow things down, and he would be fined. There was a record, exactly which order was loaded by whom and on which date.

He kept going around the shelves, checking the numbers and stuffing the envelopes. The plan was made very quickly. He already knew where the cameras were located and what they caught – this was one of the first things the Poles revealed to him. There were "dead points" where the guys used to hide for a drink during working hours. He stood with his back to the camera and deftly tucked the envelope with the dress into his jumpsuit. He continued driving around until he reached the bathroom doors. Without hurrying, he got off the cart and walked carelessly towards them. He entered and locked the door. There were no cameras here. He opened the envelope and examined the abominable dress. Then he peed on it amply and with pleasure. Then he blew his nose and smeared the snot on the inside of the collar.

He dried it with the hand dryer. The material was synthetic and dried in no time. He sniffed it, it smelled nasty. He folded it and put it back in the envelope. He hoped the bitch would put it on like this, without washing it.

During the next two days he was in an excellent mood. He learned the Dutch cases and the difference between boven and beneden[8], he was doing so well that his boss even praised him.

***

Svetoslava Tatcheva paid the courier and impatiently tore open the gray plastic envelope. The dress was not the same as at the picture on the website. It was only now she saw how cheap the fabric was, but still, from a distance it looked fine. She will like it, perhaps.

Just a year ago, she never thought that she and Lenche[9] would become friends. Lenche was just an ordinary hairdresser, and she, Mrs. Tatcheva, had a degree in literature, after all! Also, Lenche's son was one of the lazy ones. He studied only to prevent himself falling asleep, but he had big claims. She met Lenche because of him. Lenche had come to her to ask her not to fail Boris, not to prevent him from graduating. Tatcheva refused her – enough of giving a chance to idiots and lazy people! She was embarrassed

---

[8] *boven/beneden* – up/down (Dutch)
[9] *Lenche* – a pet name of the female name Elena.

enough by the case with Simon, the whole town was talking about it. But she could do nothing when his father openly threatened her. For a long time she was afraid to go back home in the evening because of him. But Lenche was not dangerous. She was a well-mannered woman, really. Tatcheva felt sorry for her, but... She met her by chance in the supermarket two days after Boris had left for the Netherlands. They talked, she tried to reassure Lenche that this was for his own good, that he would become a responsible man, he would learn to organize his life and work. Lenche agreed with a subdued face, but the sadness did not disappear from her eyes.

Tatcheva invited her for a cup of coffee. Three days later they met for coffee again, and on Sunday, too. It turned out that they had a lot in common, they started visiting each other and watching movies together.

Tatcheva regularly asked Lenche about Boris and sent him greetings. Lenche never forwarded them to him, telling her that Boris hated her and blamed her for his failures. But Tatcheva's conscience was clear. Once, Lenche shared with her, with a sigh, how she was going to redo her sister's dress in order to dress up for a relative's wedding, and Tatcheva quickly made a decision. She hadn't given gifts to anyone for years but she would for her new friend. She looked at several sites, chose a spectacular dress that was discounted, and ordered it.

***

Boris stared at the photo on his phone for a long time, thinking it was some optical illusion. His mother was holding a glass, her hair was beautiful. "Hi. I'm here at your cousin Tony's wedding. They were very sorry that you were not here. Kisses!"

Fear

Dorina looked at herself in the mirror for the hundred-and-first time. She turned the lamp off. Then she turned it back on. Then she turned around to see also her back.

She should have refused! She had to come up with something, to postpone...
But she wanted it too, didn't she?...
No, this would be the end...
But why the end? If he loved her, then he loved her...

That bluish capillary cobweb around her ankles! It was so ugly!...
Well, at least her hands were beautiful – with their pale skin and scarlet manicure...
But with brown spots, too...

But above all, never let him take off her bra! Or he must do so in the dark. God, what breasts she had in the past...

But in this "past" she flippantly gave her beautiful breasts, her beautiful legs, beautiful skin, and everything to Tony. The Idiot Drunkard Tony. And now only crumbs were left for Andrey.

Tony has been thrown away long time ago now, their kids have gone their own ways long ago; she has stopped working like a freak twelve hours a day, seven days a week to survive, also a long time ago. All her spring and all her summer she lived with proudly pressed lips, alone, tight as a coiled spring. After the bitter Tony, after the ten-year-nightmare-marriage of beating, drinking, scandals, and misery, she decided to cross the men out of her life. She'd manage better on her own! And she managed. She raised her children alone, she ran a business alone. Now she had a beauty salon and four girls worked for her. And autumn was knocking at her door.

At first she didn't realize that Andrey was He. It came via a chance meeting in a random café. He was natural, with an unconventional sense of humor; grizzled, with a little extra weight and with strong fingers. A very nice person. The chats with him were sweet, after that she always went home somehow light, cheerful, calm.

Gradually and unobtrusively, he began taking care of her – drove her car to the mechanics, did small repairs at her home, took her to interesting shows, organized surprise picnics. The last memories of such care had sunk back into the darkness of her past. Way back in her past, in childhood. And the caring man was her father.

Andrey did not make any hints about sex. This comforted and disturbed her in equal measure.

Because, she realized, she was falling in love. It scared her. She deliberately increased the distance between them and tried to look at him with the eyes of a stranger. She hoped she would find something of Tony in him every moment, so that she could say with relief and bitterness, "No, there's no point." But Andrey inevitably looked at her with his cheerful, sincere eyes. His warmth enveloped her like a blanket, she felt cozy and calm.

He also had suffered, of course. But he did not bathe in his suffering, didn't wave it like a flag, and didn't wait for sympathy. "No one is to blame for me," he used to say.

They liked different types of films but they liked to go to the cinema together, because afterwards they spent two or three pleasant hours in arguments about the movie. He touched her for the first time in the cinema. He simply put his arm over her shoulder, leaned to her, and touched her ear with his lips. "Very nice perfume," he said. All the emotions she had felt as a schoolgirl fitted into those ten seconds. She went deaf for a few moments, she tried to press herself against him, she felt hot, but most of all she felt fear.

After the cinema, they went for a drink.

"I'm not pushing you. But I really want it," he told her later, leaning across the table and taking her hand. "You know I love you. I have told you it many times."

"I know." Her throat was as dry as a book page. "Don't think I don't want it."

"Okay, you decide."

A few months passed. They met regularly, he left a pair of slippers and some clothes at hers; he even spent the night there sometimes. On the couch in the living room.

"Is there some problem?" He had hugged her waist from behind and buried his lips in her hair. She was washing vegetables at the sink.

"No. Why're you asking?"

He planted a long kiss on her neck, moved his hands down slowly, tracing her form, and stepped back. Dorina continued to wash vegetables. She scrubbed them thoroughly and didn't say anything.

Yes, it was silly. But how could she tell him that she was afraid? Dressed up, she looked great – all her friends envied her slender figure. But how could she stand naked and defenseless before him? The painful memory of the drunken Tony yelling at her, "Look at you! Get that saggy ass out of my sight!" hadn't fully disappeared from her mind. No, Andy was not like that, he would never hurt her. But the very thought of her body bringing disgust in his eyes was unbearable. Why didn't she meet him when she was twenty…

She slowly wiped her hands, took a breath, and turned around. She leaned against the sink and looked into his eyes.

"Okay, you're right. I'm being foolish." She swallowed again. "Don't stress yourself. You just turn me on just being around, and I can't help it."

"Turn you on, my eye..." She laughed shyly and lowered her gaze.

"Yes, you do. Very much," he said slowly, almost in a whisper.

"Come on, run off now or you will be late. I'll wait for you tonight." She hugged him tightly. He squeezed her.

Well, it was tonight now. In the afternoon, she visited a beautician and a manicurist. She felt like a schoolgirl before her first date — it was funny, it was abashing, but most of all, it was scary. What the hell were the steps to that dance? She couldn't remember.

Dorina looked at herself in the mirror for the hundred-and-first time. She turned the lamp off. Then she turned it back on. Then she turned around to see also her back.

She was pathetic! The expensive silk underwear hid nothing. Just exposed. Freckled neckline, neck pleats, belly stretchmarks, wide breeches and those terrible, terrible blue capillaries! All over her legs! She took the foundation makeup and began to rub it furiously into her thighs. She felt like crying. *Breathe, breathe deeply! Swallow! Once again... that's right! You won't put makeup on again!*

She wanted it, didn't she? God, how she wanted it! Her skin, her soul, were writhing for a little tenderness. Years of abstinence had not eradicated the pain. Nor the desire.

She wrapped herself tightly in her dressing gown and went to open the door.

She rested slack on his arm. Then she carefully covered her breasts with the sheet. The hairs on his skin tickled her underneath. She turned to the right, his eagle nose looked black against the moonlight. He was lying on his back with his arms under his head, his eyes open and smiling at the ceiling. She was about to ask him what he was thinking about, but she recalled the joke about the fly[10] and laughed inwardly. Then she rested her

---

[10] *A man and a woman lie in bed, he is silent and looks at the ceiling. She thinks, "Why doesn't he talk to me? He must be tired of me already... or he has someone else... or he is angry with me for something... or his mother has spoken against me again...", and she starts to cry. During this time, the man looks at the fly on the ceiling and thinks, "How come the flies stay upside down on the ceiling and don't fall down?"*

head comfortably under his shoulder and closed her eyes. God, how sweet he smelled!

Hitchhiking

Nicky was in a great mood. His new car was purring like a kitten, he was on vacation starting tomorrow, and he had just eaten his favorite sandwich at the gas station. The coffee cup swayed slightly in its holder, the radio was playing evergreens, fresh air was blowing from the air conditioner. Nicky didn't realize he had started whistling in time with the music.

Next to the detour sign, a girl was sitting on a small suitcase, waving wearily at passing cars. No, she was not one of the "professionals" working along the road.[11] She looked more like a cute college girl who was obviously going home for the holidays. Nicky hit the brakes and pulled off the road. Then he put shifter

---

[11] One can see prostitutes (even minors) along the roads very often in Bulgaria; they wave to the drivers, and then "cater" for them right in their cars.

in reverse and drove back to the girl. She perked up, got up quickly and grabbed her suitcase.

"Where are you going?"
"To Smolyan.[12] And you?"
"Right there! Get in."

Nicky glanced at his companion from time to time. Did these girls have no fear? Or did they just not care? He tried to talk to her, she answered yes/no, and after ten minutes fell asleep. Her head began to bob from side to side as he drove around the bends. Nicky felt a bit disappointed. He wanted to have a light, pleasant conversation, even flirt innocently with the beauty. He expected the whole world to share his great mood.

After Pamporovo,[13] the girl suddenly opened her eyes.

"Stop quickly, please. I'm feeling sick."

Nicky deftly swerved to the right and switched on his hazard lights. He looked ahead discreetly, then began to rummage through his phone as she threw up in the roadside ditch. Yes, it happened to almost everyone who was not used to traveling round bends. Nicky chuckled inwardly. This never happened to him.

---

[12] Smolyan is a town in Southern Bulgaria, in the mountains, the road to it is with many bends.
[13] Pamporovo is a winter resort in Rodhopi mountains.

The girl returned to the car, sat back tiredly on the seat, and apologized.

"No, no, it's okay, it's normal. Do you feel better now?"
"Yes, thank you. That's why I wanted to sleep while we were traveling so I wouldn't feel sick, but..."
"Relax, we're almost there. I will drive more slowly."

Shortly before Smolyan, the girl turned pale and said that she felt sick again. Nicky pulled over again, she got off again and threw up in the ditch again. When she returned, she looked exhausted and still very pale.

"If you're not feeling well, I should drive straight to the hospital, eh?"
"No, there's no need," the girl's voice was almost a whisper.

At that moment she closed her eyes and passed out. She slipped down the seat and Nicky got a real fright. He ran to the other side of the car, opened the door and lifted her back into the seat. He slapped her lightly on the cheeks, but she didn't react.

"Girl, hey, girl!" In his panic he couldn't remember her name, although she had introduced herself when she had got in.

He slapped her a few more times, a bit harder; her cheeks turned slightly rosy. He saw that she was breathing and he calmed down. Damn it! He got himself in trouble with that girl. Now he was not able to leave her at the first gas station in town. He decided to take her to the hospital.

In the ER they were bored and effective. Nicky sat anxiously in the waiting room while the girl was being tested inside. Somehow it wasn't right for him to walk away and leave her just like that. He had to find out what was wrong with her and, if she needed it, do something for her. He decided not to call Tanya, not to bother her unnecessarily. Also, Tanya was jealous. She would start an endless interrogation about who this girl was, what she was doing in his car, how long they had been traveling together, and so on. She wouldn't believe that he had simply succumbed to the impulse of his good mood and in a burst of generosity had decided to help the poor girl.

"Is it you who brought Mariyana Yanakieva? You can come in to see her."

Nicky was startled and looked up. A lady administrator from the hospital was standing next to him.

"Yes, thank you," he said, standing up. "Where is she?"
"Room number three. Congratulations."

Nicky walked automatically to the room without registering and processing the administrator's last word. He walked in and saw the girl sitting on a bed, a system plugged into her left arm.

"Congratulations, your girlfriend is pregnant," smiled the young doctor while writing in Mariyana's file.

"What?"
"Feeling sick is quite normal, especially while traveling around bends. Let her lie down here a bit more, and then you can take her home. And no stress, no strain anymore!"
"Wait, wait, you are mistaken, doctor. I don't know this girl. I just offered her a ride. She felt sick in the car and I brought her here."

The young doctor looked at Nicky in surprise. He then looked at the girl with a question in his eyes.

"Don't do that," Mariyana almost whispered, her eyes downcast, with blushing cheeks. "It's the worst moment and way to get rid of me."

Nicky couldn't believe her ears.

"Are you crazy?" Turning to the doctor, "Doctor, I don't know what she is talking about! I didn't even remember her name until the administrator told me!" Then he turned back to the girl, "Look, I don't know what your game is, but it sucks and it won't work!"

The girl answered nothing, only burst into tears. The doctor judgingly gave Nicky a hostile look.

"I don't know her at all, don't you understand!" Nicky raised his voice, almost shouting. "My father was so right to tell me that no good deed goes unpunished! I gave her a lift shortly after Plovdiv, she was sitting on a suitcase next to a sign and I felt sorry for her!"

"Okay, sir, take it easy. There are plenty of ways to prove that you are not the father of her child."

"I'm to prove it? Let her prove her phantasmagorias! Heavens, that came out of the blue..." And with a flurry Nicky angrily left the room, slamming the door behind him.

When at last he got home, there was no trace of his good mood. Oh, dear! Let this nonsense never reach Tanya's ears! Smolyan was such a small town, damn it. Jealous as she was, Tanya could burn him to ashes with just talk.

Thankfully the next day Nicky and his family left on their vacation to Greece and the idiotic incident faded from his mind.

At the Smolyan hospital, the young doctor in the ER was a discreet person, however the duty nurse was not. She was a bored, curious, and chatty old spinster whose only real enjoyment was learning spicy secrets. And when she couldn't learn them, she made them up. And so the story of the pregnant hitchhiker was quickly embellished and retold a dozen times to colleagues and patients.

After a week Nicky, Tanya, and their three children returned from Greece, to an unpleasant surprise. Little Smolyan, dozing in the summer heat, had become visibly amused by the spicy story. Hard times had come for Nicky. To say that Tanya caused him a scandal, would be an understatement. "Scandal" was too mundane and unrefined a word to describe the uncontrollable flow of lava pouring down on his poor head from all sides.

Tanya defiantly packed three suitcases and left with the three children for her mother in the neighboring district. Nicky clenched his teeth and decided to just wait for her anger to melt. It usually happened within two or three days. But this time things turned for the worse. Tanya kept talking. With her mother, with her sister, with her colleagues, with her hairdresser, with the workers at the gas stations and the cashiers in the supermarkets. She described Nicky as a lusty satyr with flashing eyes, his mouth drooling.

"You're not safe either!" She usually finished her tirade in front of some old lady neighbor. "Despite being over sixty, my anger is capable of anything, I'm telling you!"

Things got out of control. Tanya did not let the children see him "because he could do something to them as they were girls." She called his friends and colleagues to ask them about his movements, his doings, and most of all "with which bitch" he was doing everything. He was told to hire a lawyer because she was going to file for divorce.

Nicky didn't know what to do. His friends knew what Tanya was like and believed him to be innocent, but his bosses at the office began to view him badly. Unfortunately, his superior was a woman, and he felt a sudden change in her attitude. He tried to talk to her, but she looked at him coldly, "I didn't expect this from you, Mr. Raev. There are boundaries that should not be crossed."

"I haven't crossed any boundaries," Nicky said, trying to defend himself. "These are all stories spread by my jealous wife."

However, she didn't believe him. Stefan, his best friend, advised him to take a DNA test. "This is how you will put an end of the whole saga," he told him.

"I doubt it."

"Well, then Tanya will see in writing that the baby is not yours, and she will have to give up. Definitely."

Nicky thought once, then twice, then once more, and finally decided to do it. It would cost him a lot of trouble, but after all, he was on the verge of losing his family over that idiot girl! He went to the Emergency Room, explained to them what he wanted, and they helped him very willingly. After all, the entire ER staff was aware of the exciting saga that had begun in their rooms. Even the doctors and nurses began to bet on whether the child would end up being his or not.

"It's not his, no doubt. If it was, would he have asked for a DNA test?"

"But he decided to divorce and marry the girl, didn't you hear? So he wants a test to officially recognize the baby..."

"Um... he's quite wealthy. He could pay for whatever DNA test he'd like..."

"Nonsense. There will be a triple expertise..."

Nicky tried to seek out the cheeky hitchhiker, but he was unsuccessful. It turned out that her permanent address was in Pleven,[14] she had nothing to do with Smolyan. Nicky even went to Pleven, but no one had heard of her at the address he was given. It seemed ridiculous to him to walk around with a picture of her, asking people if they had seen her. And he had no picture of her.

---

[14] Pleven is a town in Northern Bulgaria.

Then, on a whim, he asked the police for help. He explained them the situation and they were able to track her down.

Nicky met the girl in a cafe at a gas station near Sofia. She looked somewhat larger, her pregnancy was already showing.

"Why did you play this dirty trick on me?" he asked her coldly.

She hadn't been able to refuse the meeting because she had received a summons from the court. She looked at him, embarrassed and stubborn.

"I was desperate."

"And now I am desperate," he replied meanly. "Do you know what troubles you have caused me! Do you know that my wife left me and wants a divorce? I haven't seen my kids in over a month! My bosses already consider me unreliable!"

"I'm sorry," Mariyana looked straight into his eyes, but there was not much regret in them. "I didn't do it to cause you trouble. I just wanted someone to help me."

"Then you had just to tell me! I would have helped you!"
"Will you help me now?"
"You don't lack impudence, though."

"Look, I'm not going to bore you with the sad story of my life and to list the stupid things I've done in it. I'm just asking for help. I'll do the DNA test so you can sort out the mess in your life, and you'll give me some money to rent a place for a year."

"Listen, you will do the DNA test because the court obliges you! How dare you ask me for money! I have to sue you and ask *you* for money for moral damages!"

"Okay. I know you're right and perfect, and I'm a dumb bitch who's slept with who knows who." Her dark eyes stared at him persistently, their corners were filled with tears. "I'm just begging you! Show humanity."

Nicky didn't feel like arguing. Deep in his soul he felt sorry for her. Poor little douchebag. He didn't promise her anything, they just made an appointment for the test. Just in case, he requested a double test, although only the blood test would have been sufficient.

It took a month for the results to come out. During this time, Nicky tried on several occasions to reconcile with Tanya, but to no avail. He didn't tell her he had taken a DNA test. He wanted to shove it in her face, to start a counter-scandal of revenge. He rehearsed the words he would use to force her to apologize to him, and foretasting her humiliation in the coming months.

Finally the test arrived. With a dry mouth, Nicky opened the envelope. Not that he expected the baby to be his. But the end of this long agony was in his hands. Two pages full of unintelligible medical terms, tables, and words in Latin. The most important thing was at the bottom: "The fetus in the 24th gestational week of Mariyana Yanakieva has a 100% mismatch with the genetic material from Nikolay Raev." Yes! He carefully folded the paper again along the same folds, slipped it into the envelope, and with jubilation bubbling in his chest, took the phone out of his pocket. Then he stopped. No, he won't call Tanya. He will simply give the results to his lawyer, who will give them to her lawyer. He only desperately wanted to catch a glimpse of her face from somewhere while she would be reading it.

Then he paid attention to the second sheet in the envelope. He opened it and read it absentmindedly. More incomprehensible Latin terminology. "... viable sperm – 0. Conclusion: Complete and irreversible sterility. Reasons: Unclear".

Nicky read the paper several times, turned it over, but there was nothing more written on the other side. He looked at the top, saw his name, even his social security number. He read the entire sheet carefully once more. "Viable sperm – 0".

Whose, on earth, were his three beautiful daughters then?

Assembling

"A cup of coffee?" She looked at him from above her reading glasses.

"No, thanks".

She turned back to the desk and adjusted her glasses. A loud clatter of keys was heard again. He proceeded to take boards out of the cartons and to arrange them in piles around him.

After a while she looked at him over her glasses again. He worked quickly and skillfully. He took out screws from some bags, put one board on top of another, then put it away, then checked something in the drawing, then looked for another board. Despite the rush, he didn't seem worried or in a hurry. She enjoyed watching the measured movements of his long, thin fingers. He wasn't looking at her, his long hair was falling over his eyes, but he didn't seem to mind.

Their eyes accidentally met. He smiled.

"I know, it looks a bit messed up. But everything will be alright."

She smiled, too. She had a nice smile, her whole face was smiling. The tiny wrinkles around her eyes were visible.

"I never doubted it."
"I thought, you were afraid that I am ruining your nice bookcase."
"Ha-ha-ha! No! On the contrary, you work very skillfully."
"Thank you. It's not something difficult. I'm used to it."

She got up from her chair and walked towards him. She was petite, with a little belly and thin ankles.
"Don't step here barefoot, you might prick yourself on something."

She stopped, took her glasses off her nose and scratched her head.

"I thought, I could help you if you want me to."
"No, there's no need. I told you, I'm used to it. If you help me, you'll only slow me down."

She looked at him for a while and said:

"Well, I'll make some coffee. I'll drink a cup anyway".

"Okay then."

"How do you like it?"

"Make it as you make yours."

She walked to the kitchen and he followed her with his eyes. When looked at from behind, she appeared younger. Well, the soft waistband gave something away, but she still looked nice. Her reddish hair was casually pulled up at neck with a patterned hairband, and her short sleeves exposed nicely tanned arms.

"Excuse me for staring at you like that a moment ago, but you are a very pleasant sight. I haven't seen a young man working so skillfully and competently for a long time. I'm already used to seeing the young people only in cafes, busy doing nothing."

"Well, I can't afford to be like that."

"You're married, perhaps?"

"No."

"A girlfriend?"

He remained silent for a moment.

"Sort of."

"A cute definition."

He remained silent for a second time.

"I'm sorry, these are personal issues, of course. I'm such a curious auntie."

"No, no problem. I'm just… I am not aware of myself lately."

"Welcome to the club," she said in good English. He looked at her with a surprise.

"Well, at my age I'm supposed to be aware by now, but..." His last words were lost in the sudden roar of the drill. He was not looking at her, but had assumed an awkward position, underlaying one board with his left knee and pressing another one to the ground with his right.

"Well, 'your age' still allows for some disorientation." She sat down on the nearest stool and rested her elbows on her knees. With her left hand she held the saucer and with her right, the cup of coffee. "Do you plan to study something or do you like your craft?"

He checked that the holes matched, inserted a screw and pulled the trigger on the machine. When the howling died down, she continued:

"Sorry, I started questioning you again. Excuse me. I do it involuntarily."

"No, no problem. I just can't do two things simultaneously. If I start answering you, I'll drive the screw wrong."

He stood up, dusted off his knees and reached for the cup.

"Thanks for the coffee. I'm actually graduating this year. I interrupted my studies twice because I had to work. I support myself", he added shyly.

"Congratulations!" There was such admiration in her voice that he looked at her with interest. "Indeed, I congratulate you. You must be a member of a very rare, disappearing breed. What are you studying?"

"Interior architecture."

"So you are almost working on your specialty." She laughed.

"Yes, I get acquainted with the business from bottom to top. And I learned the craft from my father."

"But you also have talent. You are very skilled."

"Thanks. As long as it was a compliment," he added after a short pause.

"It is a compliment, of course! If I had a daughter, I'd take you as my son-in-law." She laughed again with whole her face, the tiny wrinkles around her eyes becoming even more visible.

"You can hardly have a daughter at this age." He felt obliged to give a compliment back.

"You accumulate red points at a champion pace! You even know how to give compliments! Maybe, you are 45 years old and your age doesn't show?"

"Now I really don't know if that was a compliment."

"From my lips – yes. Sorry, but I'm finding it increasingly difficult to find guys of your generation I can have a decent conversation with. And yes, I have sons almost your age."

"No way!" This time the surprise in his voice was absolutely sincere.

"No way, you say, but it's a fact." She stood up and took the cups to the kitchen. When she returned, she sat down at the computer again and put on her glasses. "I won't bother you anymore, you're busy."

"How I wish my girlfriend would reason like you!" He was sitting in the chair across her and was looking at her over the lid of the open laptop. They were having a second cup of coffee.

"About what?"

"She is ashamed that I do manual work and support myself. She doesn't let me mention it when we are out."

"Why?" The genuine surprise was in her voice this time.

"Because her parents somehow instilled in her that it is more chic not to work, but simply *to have money*. Not that they are very rich, they have some little grocery store in Chepelare[15], but they raised her like a grand dame. She lives in a luxurious studio apartment in Lozenets[16], drives a Mini Cooper to lectures, goes to manicure and pedicure every week... things like that. On the other hand, she is very smart, sweet, and has a good soul, but we cannot reach an

---

[15] Chepelare (Чепеларе) – a small town in Southern Bulgaria
[16] Lozenets (Лозенец) – a prestigious district of Sofia

agreement concerning work and money."

"What does she study?"

"Psychology."

"A serious science."

"Come on! She studies for prestige. I told you, she is very smart and easily passes her exams; she has a memory of a devil. But she doesn't plan to work at all. She developed some theory – how she would rent out properties and never work. She constantly tells me that I'm getting dumb from doing this work."

"She is getting dumb!" Her voice was sharp and her eyes were wide with anger. "Look, I don't know her, but I'm telling you, run away from her! A woman who thinks about manicures and tanning salons all day is the worst possible partner in life."

"The problem is, I can't stand sloven women. Ever since I was little, I've been obsessed with refined, spiffy women. To me, this is a sign of intelligence and culture."

"Yes, and topped with a generous dose of egoism, in addition."

"Well, you can't do without it."

"And you want to live with an egoist?"

"I'm ready to swallow it, I guess."

"And your children one day?"

He looked at her with embarrassment, as if she had peeked into his messy room.

"It's too early to think about that."

"Sure... sorry, I'm meddling in your business again."

She put her glasses back on and returned to the screen. He felt that he had disappointed her, and for some reason he didn't want to. Strangely enough, he knew he was disappointing Rennie all the time (she didn't want to be referred to by her real name, Raina; it made him laugh when he thought about it), but it didn't really bother him, he had accepted it as a part of the scenery. But now, to disappoint this strange woman seemed unbearable to him. He desperately wanted to make a good impression.

"Do your sons live with you?" he asked after an awkward pause, more informally now.

"No, they are abroad. They study and support themselves. Just like you." Her voice was reserved, but still, she looked at him over her glasses.

"So, you live alone?"

"Why do you assume so?"

"Well..." Now he was really embarrassed and didn't know what to answer.

"Because I called a craftsman to assemble my bookcase? Or because no one could bear such a prying, omniscient auntie?" There was still a bit of sarcasm in her voice, but there was a little fun in it now. He sensed the truce.

"Oh, please! I never said that. But the bookcase is an argument, admit it," he added after a short pause.

"My husband is a photographer and travels a lot. Otherwise, he is much more skilled than you and would have assembled this bookcase by now. But that would mean I would have to jump over the boxes for two more weeks until he got home. And I work from home, and I would get nervous. And now I'll surprise him, in addition."

"Sure. Well, I have one more part to assemble and I'm done. Thanks for the coffee."

"If you're hungry, I can make something for you."

"No thanks." She felt the hesitation in his voice.

"Relax, I can cook. Do you like spaghetti?"

"I like everything."

"Okay, finish this here and I'll do it in the meantime. I am hungry, too."

"Okay, thanks." And he took the drill. He didn't know why but her invitation excited him immensely, he couldn't wait to sit at the same table with her. A premonition of some important experience came over him.

"Excuse me, why did you react like that a while ago?"

"When?"

"When we were talking about my girlfriend."

"Forget it, it was none of my business."

"No, I'm curious."

"Leave it, I shouldn't have started. It doesn't concern me. It's just that I have sons almost at your age and I'm struggling to understand your way of thinking."

"Is it so important for everything to be perfect?"

"Excuse me?"

"Perfect. You want everything to be perfect. Even if it doesn't concern you."

She laughed briefly and put down the fork.

"Maybe psychology is contagious? Actually, you know…" She put her elbows on either side of the plate. "Nothing could be further from the truth! I am the most imperfect person in the world. I have a bunch of flaws, some of which I'm still in the process of uncovering."

"Such as?" His voice was quiet and careful.

"Such as, I usually miss the moment", she shook her head and turned back to the spaghetti. "I don't appreciate how important are the things I have right now. I'm constantly waiting for something good, I'm afraid of something bad, I think about tomorrow, about the next summer, about old age…" She looked thoughtfully at her plate and rolled the spaghetti on her fork. "And the point is to feel the moment, to experience it, to absorb it and to keep it forever."

He ate very quietly, scared that some sudden sound could interrupt the stream.

"I was once in Chalkidiki. On a huge, deserted beach. And for half an hour I experienced fullness. I don't know whether you understand me. It was an absolute indulgence for all the senses. A complete bliss." Her voice died away, her eyes closed, her hand still kept mechanically rolling the fork. Her fingers were fine, with telltale brown spots here and there.

"Has this ever happened to you?" She suddenly opened her eyes and looked at him with curiosity. "Just like that, to experience a moment in which you say to yourself: 'Now, here, in this moment, I feel complete bliss'?"

"I guess it hasn't. Or if it has, I failed to register it."

"You see, that's the problem. We miss. This is one of my biggest flaws. I miss. And then I regret it. But I didn't miss that moment. At least that one."

"Describe it to me."

He expected some sort of embarrassment, withdrawal, closing in her shell. So did most of the women he had communicated with. They worried about their perfection. They thought he liked them with halos. And she only looked at him with curiosity.

"Are you really interested? This is my nonsense."

"Yes, I am a lot. Cross my heart. I've been thinking about the same things lately. I guess, I have the same flaw."

"Okay." She laid her fork down again, put her elbows on the table and leaned forward. "It was a conscious, purposeful registration of sensations. I was just lying there on the sand, feeling the warmth of the sun. I could feel the wind turning the hairs on my arms, tickling my ears, and I said to myself, 'This is complete sensory bliss.' I watched the sun and the clouds, the gray-white light on the water, a pair of seagulls flying in perfect synchrony, as if someone was leading them by a common rope; I watched how the sea lived, moved, breathed, and I asked myself: 'Is there a more beautiful sight than this?' And I answered: 'No, there is not. So, this is total visual bliss.' I listened to the splashing of the sea, the distant music, and the scraping of pebbles as the waves receded — a noise I could listen to forever. Auditory bliss. And finally I breathed in the aroma with a full chest. My favorite scent – sea, wind, juniper, herbs, sun-toasted stones. Something like that..." she finished and leaned back to the spaghetti.

He wanted to swallow, but couldn't. He felt like if he did, he would burst into tears. With all his soul he wanted to live with this woman for the rest of his life. And he felt literal physical pain at the thought that it wouldn't happen. She noisily sucked the last strand of spaghetti and licked her lips.

"You didn't like my cooking, I guess?"
"No, no..." He was startled. "I was just thinking."

She was old, for God's sake! She could have been his mother. Almost. Her neck was seared and the roots of her hair were white.

When she moved with her back to him, he could see the dilated capillaries around her ankles. *She didn't look bad in clothes, but... Actually, she had a manicure, too!* Now he noticed. He looked at her feet. *And a pedicure! She just didn't talk about them! She had other topics to talk about.*

"It must have sounded crazy to you. But I prefer not to miss such things. Life is too short. Before me I have less life left than I have behind me. I started the second season of my life. And I feel sorry for the missed nice episodes of the first season."
"Aren't you worried about what I'll think of you when you talk like that?"

She laughed again with her beautiful laugh.

"I stopped worrying about what people think of me a long time ago. But it took me a lot of time and pain to realize that it was the right thing to do. That's why I reacted the way I did to your girlfriend's dreams of a carefree parasitic life, in which the biggest concern is not to break your manicure. I myself had such a period and I am ashamed of it. I am ashamed of what my selfishness has done to my husband and my sons. Thank God, I realized myself in time, so that the damage was not fatal."

She carried the plates to the sink and began cutting fruit, with her back to him. She put the pieces in the blender.

"Do you like strawberries?"

"I do."

"Do you know what is the most important of all feelings?" She kept silent and he wondered what an answer she was expecting.

"Love?"

"Love is too blurred and a very commercialized concept today. Every hormonal urge is considered love. Don't make me read you treatises on love now."

"Then what?"

"Gratitude! Most important of all is to be grateful! Gratitude means happiness!"

She started the blender and waited for it to grind the fruit. Then she took out two large cups and poured the liquid in them in equal parts. She pushed one of them towards him.

"To be grateful means to realize what you have; to think about it and not about what you don't have. To be grateful means to have good feelings about people. To be grateful means to fully experience such moments. Here, now, I am grateful. A lot."

"To whom?"

"First of all to you – for assembling my bookcase so nicely; for being such a nice and polite young man. You could have been some noisy bounder who would have smelled up my whole apartment with his cigarettes. And who would throw cynical remarks at me. And you are such a kind, smart and decent young man."

He blushed.

"Oh, dear! You shouldn't give thanks for such things!"
"Of course, I should. Second, I thank God that he had sent you, that we had such an interesting conversation, that you loved my spaghetti. I appreciate this moment and put it in the storage of my precious experiences."
"I think, I should thank you." His voice was quiet, his eyes were fixed on the table.
"Okay, it's good that we are grateful to each other."

Actually, he thought while driving through the afternoon traffic, *God knew his business. If this woman could bear me children and if she was single... Rennie just wouldn't have a chance.*

His phone rang.

"Yes, kitty."
"You haven't forgotten about tonight, have you?"
"I haven't, kitty."
"And please say you're coming from the gym or something. Don't mention your crappy job. I don't want them to think I got a boyfriend from the country."

"I won't come, kitty."

"Why?"

"Because I can't."

"But you promised me!" The voice from the other side raised an octave.

"I know, I'm sorry. But I have one more site to go, and I'll be done. I won't be good company. And stop calling my work 'crappy'."

"Oh, I'm sick of that! I always wonder what to think of, to justify your absences!"

"Well, stop wondering. Just say that your boyfriend is a serious man and works to support himself, and does not rely on mom and dad."

"You're impossible!"

"Yeah, bye." And he hung up.

Traffic Jam

Last chance indeed. There will be no other.

So many lies were told, so many disappointments were swallowed, so much mistrust was accumulated... This time the promise must be kept. "I'll be with you at ten." That's what he had promised her and he would be with her, whatever would happen.

He left early, to avoid the morning traffic. At seven o'clock he was already on the highway.[17] The sun rose above the mountains and shone directly into his eyes.

It will be like this forever? For the rest of their lives? The tension somewhere between his stomach and diaphragm never went away

---

17 The story takes place on the *Trakia* highway, which links Sofia with the Black Sea through Southern Bulgaria. The mentioned locations are there.

even for a moment during those sixteen months. He knew what he wanted, he knew he wanted her; he knew she wanted him, too. But the tension did not disappear even for a second. Fear... that he would not understand her desire in time; that she would not take his joke; that he would be late for a date; that he would find her in an unexpected mood; that uninvited people would show up; that she would appear to him disagreeable and vulgar; that he would seem to her disagreeable and vulgar...

He hadn't imagined it like that. He had expected some light-hearted calmness and mutual understanding only with looks; ceaseless laughter and tickling; mad giggling and quick forgiveness; and above all – no tension. The thought of such tension for the rest of his life was like a thorn under his fingernail. But still, he didn't want to lose her. He didn't imagine any scenario of separation.

Last night it happened again. Long whining accusations on the phone. Repetitive explanations; humiliating excuses. He promised that he would come, and until they cleared everything up, he wouldn't leave.

"You won't come, I know it. You'll call me again at 'ten to...' to tell me you have an important engagement."
"I'll come. I have no more important engagement than you."

"I hope you are sure. Because you know... my trust in you is thinned to a hair's breadth. I can't take one more disappointment. This will be the last one."

How come she always managed to put him on his knees? Why he was the one who kept apologizing and making promises every time? That nasty tension again.

"I promised you, right? If I don't come, then you can grumble."

"No, I won't grumble. I'll just disappear from your life. For real."

"Don't say that. Let's not get nervous now on the phone. We'll talk calmly, face to face tomorrow. Wait for me at ten."

Should he call her, tell her he's already on his way? No, he'll wake her up. She must still be sleeping. Besides, there was no need to report as a student before her. He will arrive exactly at ten and that's it. A word of a man.

After he passed the Trajan's Gate Tunnel, he increased his speed. He descended toward the valley, the sun already high enough to hide it behind the visor. He looked at the car's clock – fifteen to eight. He would be in Plovdiv even before nine, no doubt. He would even have time to drink a cup of coffee and to organize his defense speech. Absently, he turned on the radio. The tension began to dissipate.

So, what? The worst thing that could happen is that they break up.

No, it will hardly come to that. They're not sixteen-year-old teens, after all. They will come to an agreement like mature people.

A few kilometers after the exit to Pazardzhik, the brake lights of the cars in front of him suddenly came on. He was startled and jumped on the brake. He worriedly looked in the rear-view mirror. Thank God, the car behind him was far enough away. He almost hit the red Renault in front of him! Both lanes filled up with cars in seconds. After a while, they set off in fits and starts. He tried to see what was going on in front but couldn't. Five meters, stop... ten meters, stop... three meters, stop... He expected to see a car accident or something like that after a while, but there was none. Half an hour... forty minutes... thank God he had left early!

At some point it seemed to him that in the adjacent lane the queue was moving a bit faster. He waited for a driver in it to get distracted, and deftly slipped in front of him. Now the other lane moved faster! He passed a few times a gray station wagon, full with inflated beach balls in the back. Gradually the station wagon gained a lead and got lost ahead. And he was stuck behind a bus spewing diesel fumes. He closed the windows and turned on the air conditioner, but the smell kept coming in. A German-registered van filled with headscarved women gradually caught up to him on the left.[18] Little by little it overtook him. At one point, a

---

18 Turkish families living in Germany traveling in both directions are a common sight on the *Trakia* highway.

motorcyclist passed between the two lanes and he sincerely envied him. Every few minutes, some shuffler hit the gas on the right in the emergency lane. It was for ambulances and police cars in such situations, you jerks! But the jerks didn't care. He started cursing them in his head.

He anxiously watched the clock on the dashboard, and switched radio stations in hope that something would be said regarding the cause of the delay. At twenty past ten he was not even close to Plovdiv. He realized he would have to call her. The queue in front of him moved, but the small Micra[19] in the left lane didn't. He passed it and saw a girl with big glasses at the wheel, anxiously trying to start the engine. It had died and wouldn't turn over. After a while his lane stopped again, he looked in the rear-view mirror. It was still standing there, not moving, and behind it the nervous drivers were honking their horns. He felt sorry for the girl, put on his hazard lights, got out and ran back up the lane.
"A problem?" The girl looked at him worriedly.
"It overheated and I turned it off, and now I can't start it."
"Release the gear lever, I'll push you."

He put his shoulder to the small car and pushed it with all his might. It moved a little and started rolling slowly forward. The drivers kept honking from behind. *"Hey, what a people are you! Why are you honking like this? You'd better come here and push!"*

---

19 Micra – a small car model of Nissan.

But no one joined him. He leveled with his car, even passed it. Meanwhile the queue in his lane had crept forward and his car was sitting there embarrassed – alone and naked, lights flashing. He ran back to it and drove it.

Then back to the girl.

"Get out, if you want to. Let me try."

She didn't object and hurried out. He slipped in quickly and turned the key. Ah, it had chocked. He turned the key few times briefly with no throttle. It started. He looked up and saw a smile of relief on her face.

"Thank you very much!"

"No problem. Don't put it out anymore and don't throttle it. Let the battery charge."

"Okay, thanks."

He got out and ran to his car again. He caught up with the smelly bus and stopped once more. Only now he saw that he had thrown his phone on the seat next to him. Four missed calls. The tension hit him with new force. He looked at the clock – ten fifteen. A sense of doom came over him. Well, that was it. Apparently they were not meant to be together. For a second, he felt irritated by the bespectacled girl in the Micra. If only her car hadn't fizzled out like that... what if it hadn't fizzled? Would he have got out of the traffic jam and made it in time?... Well, at least he could have rung in time... but what if he had? He would have done it just to say that he couldn't keep his word... Well, how come it's his fault that there's a traffic jam? He had no helicopter, after all!

He dialed the number with a sense of defeat.

"Hello?"

"No need. Don't bother yourself. I picked up just to tell you that you don't need to drive all the way to Plovdiv."

"Listen…"

"I was sure it would happen like this. And you know, I'm not even disappointed."

"Don't do that, I'm in traffic jam."

"No, I'm not mad at you, but don't come. I won't be at home. Delete my number from your phone."

"Why don't you want to listen to me?"

The silence was a hint that she had hung up. He dialed the number again. *"This number is currently unavailable."* Irritation, resentment, rising anger... and a microscopic drop of a sense of freedom. Satisfaction that the film ended exactly as he had predicted.

Honking from behind startled him. The smelly diesel had moved a hundred meters ahead, and he was still standing there with the phone in his hand. He applied some gas. Leveled up with the

Micra. He waved the bespectacled girl in it and rolled down the window.

"Everything alright?"

"Yes, thank you very much!"

"Drive safely!"

For a little while, they moved like this, at intervals of a hundred meters, and now she passed by him, then he passed by her. Somewhere ahead he saw flashing lights and a shift in the dense throng of cars. They were obviously approaching the cause of the traffic jam, whatever it was. But there was nowhere for him to hurry now. And there was no reason to go on to Plovdiv. At the first exit, he would turn back to Sofia. But before then, he would stop at a gas station. The two cups of coffee and the two bottles of water were urging to come out. And he was hungry.

At last! A full-length white refrigerated truck had stretched across two of the lanes. Lying on its side like a fallen albino elephant, its wheels indecently cocked and its insides shamelessly exposed. Around it, police officers and various people with phones were anxiously hurrying to and fro. He didn't see an ambulance, and that calmed him down a bit. The driver must have fallen asleep... or had a flat tire, who knows. He must have been hurrying while on his phone. There were two police cars in the emergency lane, probably waiting for a crane or something to move the corpse of the truck.

Then the traffic was suddenly unleashed. Angry with being forced to wait in the heat, the drivers nervously pressed their accelerators and each looked to sneak before the others. To the right, the silhouette of a gas station outlined. Yes, there was no rush now.

He gave a right turn signal and turned right. Apparently he wasn't the only one whose natural needs were exacerbated by the traffic jam. There was a queue outside the restroom. He headed for the restaurant at the far side of the parking lot, hoping its restroom would be more accessible. The Micra sat neatly and tamely between two huge trucks. Its tinted windows flashed. Was it the same one? He didn't remember the number plate. But the color matched.

They almost clashed at the door. She was walking out with a sandwich and a cup of coffee in her hands and trying to open the door with her foot. He was bent on only one thing – the restroom. He almost spilled her coffee.

"Oh, sorry!" He raised his hands in apology.

"It's okay, you didn't spill it."

Their eyes met and they both laughed sheepishly. Her eyes flashed silver behind her glasses.

"Oh, it's you! I'm glad we met. I failed to thank you properly. I am very ashamed my car died like that."

"No, no! It could happen to anyone."

"No, I insist on buying you a coffee at least."

The last thing he needed now was coffee.
"No, there's no need, really. Thanks. Have a pleasant and safe trip!"
"Then a sandwich?"
"No, thanks. Don't worry."

She felt him struggling to get her out of there.
"You must be in a hurry. Excuse me." She smiled with embarrassment and disappointment.
"No, I just have to visit the restroom." Now he was embarrassed.
"OMG, I'm sorry! I am so slow-witted! Okay, I'll wait for you."

He was about to say, "no need" but felt it would be rude.
"Excuse me, I'll be back in a minute."

The minute turned into more than five because there was a queue in front of this restroom as well. He even thought he wouldn't find her when he got back. But she was sitting at one of the tables outside, sipping coffee and staring absently at the parking lot.

"Sorry for the delay, there was a queue."
"It's okay. I'm in no rush."
"No way. Everyone is in a rush somewhere."

"Not me. While hanging in the traffic jam, I was told there was no point in rushing anymore."
"Same here!" He laughed out loud.

A huge truck just in front of them started its engine and they both jumped up.
"Run or fight?"

She laughed with her whole face and her full voice.
"Better run, I forgot my rifle."

They moved to another table, he also bought a sandwich and cup of coffee. He expected at any moment the tension to sprout somewhere there, in its usual place – between his stomach and his diaphragm.

It didn't sprout. She had a very contagious laugh.

Strange Choice

There were free seats in the bus, but she deliberately didn't sit. She never did. Especially in winter. The icy seats covered with crannied imitation leather foisted their cold through the woolen skirt and her thighs froze to death. The skirt happened to be wollen but it was loose and the cold was constantly blowing underneath. But if she stood upright, with her legs firmly planted together, she sensed at least some of her own warmth.

She was keeping balance in the middle of the bus, in the "hoop", leaning her back against the vertical pipe and breathing shallowly through her teeth, to sense as little as possible the stench of diesel that filled the rattly *Ikarus*.[20] Her neck was stiff with tension and

---

[20] Ikarus – public transport busses made in Hungary during the communism. The most popular model is a double long bus with a rotating "hoop" in the middle.

cold, she was staring out the dirty windows. The streets were completely dark, it was among the shortest days of the year. From time to time, streetlamps with damp orange halos flickered by. She knew by the jolt and stagger when her stop was approaching. She moved toward the door with the gait of a sailor on deck in a stormy sea.

The doors hissed open and she stepped out into an icy mess of water and snow. The bus had stopped too far from the curbstone and she was unable to jump over the puddle. She felt her left ankle boot fill with icy bone-chilling slush.

Teeth chattering and body shivering, she slipped and slid all the way home.

The first thing she did when she got indoors was change her shoes. In warm socks and slippers, she gradually began to feel her feet again. She took her dark blue uniform to her room, removed the white collar,[21] washed it by hand over the kitchen sink and hung it on the dryer above the stove. She also washed her tights, which were wet and muddy. In doing so her hands got warm. She opened the stove, it hadn't gone out. She added two logs and smiled contentedly. Now it would get really warm.

---

[21] The school uniforms for girls during the communism are black or dark-blue garments with white collars.

She found a pot with a whole sauerkraut in the sink, and a note from her mother on top: "Cook sauerkraut with rice." She was very happy. Not only would they would have sauerkraut with rice for dinner, which she adored, but her mother had taken the cabbage out from the tube, and now she didn't have to stir in the ice-cold brine![22] She cut the sauerkraut in pieces and put it on to boil.

She took the textbooks and notebooks out of her schoolbag, checked her schedule for tomorrow, and ran to her room to pack accordingly. It was freezing cold there; she got there only for night sleep. As it was in the whole house, except for the kitchen, by the way. The kitchen had an old heavy stove and it was warm. And they lived there, she, her brother, her mother and her father. It was good, all of them were out most of the day, so they didn't stay together in it for long. They only got together more or less for dinner. So she hurried to write her homework on the kitchen table before the others got home.

Checking her schedule for tomorrow, she ran to her bedroom to change her books and pack her schoolbag. Like the rest of the house, save the kitchen, it was freezing cold in there, and she usually avoided it until it was time for sleep. The kitchen

---

[22] A very popular way of preparing food for winter months was to put big wooden or plastic tubes in cold places as sheds or cellars, and fill them with cabbages in brine.

benefitted from the old heavy stove, and that was where her brother, mother, and father all gravitated upon their return home. As soon as one arrived the focus would immediately be on dinner, and so she hurried to complete her homework on the kitchen table before then.

Her mother was a pediatrician and was on duty in shifts. She would come home on the last bus at ten o'clock tonight. Her father played in the opera orchestra and they had a performance that night. He would be home around midnight, usually dropped by a colleague with a car (her family didn't have a car). Her brother was on second shift at school and would be home in about an hour. She should have finished her homework and lessons by then.

Easy thing. How easy and pleasant life would be if her biggest problem was her lessons! As it was for the rest of her classmates. They were only worried about whether they would be tested in chemistry, if there was going to be a test in mathematics, and how they would write their essays in literature. To her, these were funny trifles. The real weight in her chest came from elsewhere.

Sometimes she wondered if God had made fun of her. It was not possible for the life of an eighteen-year-old girl to have accumulated all the nasty things the twentieth century could invent. To be born not just in a small communist country, but also into a Protestant family! In two mutually exclusive universes. And on top of that, in poverty.

She learned that communism was a bad thing from her father, even before she could pronounce the word correctly. At the same time, it was explained to her that if she even once, even by accident, even with good intentions, let anyone know that her father had said such a thing, she would have a father in prison. She couldn't read yet, but she already knew how to live a double life. At school she studied poems about the party[23], took part in recitals, and was even considered an exemplary pioneer[24]. At home she listened to *Free Europe Radio*[25] with her father, and immediately closed the windows when seeing him switching on the *VEF*[26] on 13 meters shortwave[27].

She was very careful no one at school knew that she was going to church. It was the worst possible thing that could happen to her.

---

[23] The Communist Party.

[24] The Youth Communist organization for children up to 14 is called "Pioneer Organization", and its members, "pioneers".

[25] Free Europe Radio – a radio made and financed by the US government during the communism, which work is to broadcast information about the real situation in the communist countries and around the world. It is forbidden in all communist countries, and listening to it is punished by the law.

[26] VEF – small radio sets produced in Soviet Union during the communism.

[27] VEF is very popular among the people listening to illegal radio stations, as only it broadcasts in short waves, mainly 13 meter wave length.

At school, they were lectured that religion was the opium of the people and that only the simple old women in the villages go to church. She was ashamed of being a simple old woman who took opium. At the same time, she liked to go to church, she had friends there, she didn't need to live a double life there, and everyone was very friendly. The harassment they were all subjected to, the semi-legal events they organized, united them. She loved going on mountain hikes with her friends from church, climbing chukars, sitting by the fire in the evenings, humming with the others, innocently flirting with the boys.

If only her parents were not so conservative! Her mother was prone to asceticism. To do something just for pleasure was a sin. If an activity didn't have at least one practical useful application, it was considered inappropriate. If a garment had any functions other than covering the body and keeping warm, it was considered inappropriate. If a food served anything other than supplying energy to the body, it was also considered inappropriate. That's why her mother cooked almost without spices, with very little fat, and made insipid watery desserts on the rare occasions we had dessert.

Nina was a different girl! She had dimples on both cheeks and loved to laugh. She liked to eat delicious things, wear beautiful clothes, and feel pleasures. But the diabolical combination into which she had been born categorically denied her all that. Tasty things weren't on the family menu at all (unless they were healthy) and eating out was a completely unknown thing for the family. It was expensive, there were only a few restaurants in the city, and they offered "unhealthy" things. Nina learned how to cook alone, by reading cookbooks as one reads novels — with passion and intoxication. She imagined the taste of the dishes just from the description of the ingredients. But cooking remained a big challenge, simply because she could hardly find all the ingredients she needed. From the nearby grocery store, they bought what was available at the moment and what was "released"[28]. And yet, she soon became a better cook than her mother. Her mother grumbled that Nina's dishes were too fatty and too spicy, but Nina received unexpected support from her father, who lavished praise on her. And her mother quickly left the space around the sink to her, because she didn't like to cook anyway.

Beautiful clothes were out of question. She wore a school uniform[29], and her parents made it clear that they did not have money for "double" outfits – that is, for uniform clothes and for those worn outside of school. And in her high school it was a matter of honor and prestige if you were seen around town during

---

[28] Under communism, grocery stores constantly run out of basic food products, and when the store stocks up with a missing good, people say it was "released". Waiting in line for food is a daily occurrence.

[29] Wearing a school uniform is absolutely mandatory during communism. Students without uniform are not allowed to enter the school.

non-school hours, you were "natty". Well, there was no way for Nina to be natty. And in non-school hours, she still wore white blouses and black skirts, and tied some colorful scarf so that she wouldn't be made fun of for wearing a uniform outside of school. New shoes were bought when the old ones got torn.

Also, "nattying" was at odds with her family's strict Puritan religion. Anything related to "worldly vanity" was considered a terrible sin. Thus, Nina was not just in the category of "country old women using opium", but also belonged to a religious minority, considered even by traditional priests to be fanatical and harmful.

It was a pure miracle that she had girlfriends. Well, they were not great friends – none of them considered her a "best" friend, she was second or third on everyone's list, but at least she wasn't alone and isolated. She had someone to hang around with during breaks and go to the movies with. A secret she kept from her mother because the cinema was also one of the vanity pleasures. She kept her friendships at the cost of a lot of lies. She hid, invented, fantasized... She lived in an almost fictional world, which she presented to others as pure truth. She was rarely caught in a lie and almost always managed to get away with some sort of explanation.

In addition, she was a damn good student and everyone copied her homework, tests, and essays. During term tests, she wrote not only her essays, but those of at least of two other students. She never asked for anything in return, and maybe that's why some of her classmates felt obliged to at least repay her with a good attitude.

She was beautiful. Although she didn't think so at all. To her, as to almost everyone at that age, "beautiful" meant "well-dressed." And she was ugly dressed. Therefore, her athletic figure, classic features, and beautiful eyes didn't impress anyone. Including her. She envied her girl classmates who received love notes from the boys, not because she liked those boys, but because of the attention the girls received. When she received her first love note, she felt excited and flattered, even though she didn't like the boy who had sent it, at all.

This double life strained her terribly and filled her with unsatisfied irritation. From time to time, in the homes of her classmates and friends, she looked through *Neckermann* or *Burda* magazines[30] and could not believe what beautiful clothes existed in this world. She watched the movie *Rocky* at least ten times. Not because she liked boxing or sports movies. No, God forbid! But simply

---

[30] *Neckermann* is the most popular mail order company in Europe for more than 60 years. Its catalogs are smuggled into communist countries, where they enjoyed great popularity. From them, people in these countries learn what fashion looks like around the world. *Burda* is a fashion magazine with instructions on how women can sew their own clothes, in it.

because she loved the footage of Rocky running in the morning twilight between the skyscrapers with beautiful music in the background. What wonderful cities there are in the world! She loved both French and Italian films, simply because they showed streets, cafes, shops, and houses from another world. The world her father said was the real one, and they lived in the nightmare one. Most of all she liked to watch the comedies of Louis de Funes because they were funny, because the people there drove nice cars, wore nice clothes and lived in nice houses.

Her father had colleagues who had emigrated to the West, from whom he heard this and that. Even from time to time he brought home some chocolate brought "from outside". Nina and her brother shared it to the last crumb and ate it like Holy Communion.

While quickly solving the organic chemistry equations she had for homework, she kept thinking. But he couldn't find an answer. Three unpleasant things were coming her way, and she wondered which ones she could avoid, if any at all, and how. It was as if three nasty iron weights had pressed down on her stomach.

First, she had to somehow inform her folks that they were collecting money for the New Year's party at school. Every year there were arguments about this in her family. "You won't go to any stupid parties!" her mother usually snapped. But Nina insisted that it was mandatory, otherwise she would be written absent. In fact, she wouldn't be, but she insisted she would. She was constantly absent from any gatherings where the people had to be "natty", anyway. Because she had nothing to put on. Now the party would be after classes, so everyone would be in uniform. And she desperately wanted this time to be like the others, not to have to come up with stupid excuses, but to do what the others do.

"They know only one thing to do – to ask for money!" her father muttered. "Tell them we don't have any."
Well, that was something she would never tell them, even if she had to bite her tongue off. Communism or not – in her elite high school it was shameful to be poor and say you had no money. And she had been telling and fantasizing a lot about her father's business trips abroad and her imaginary relatives in different countries. "I can't. Everyone will give money", she used to answer. In the end, of course, they would give her money, but accented with it meaning the crossing out of her New Year's gift. She would agree, but later would have to think of gifts she had received, to tell her classmates. Now she had the same battle ahead of her, maybe even worse, because yesterday her brother had asked for money for the same thing and got it after a big argument. She was afraid they would take it out on her, and would make up for what they had spent on her brother by saving on her.

The second unpleasant thing was the upcoming "battle" with the history teacher. He was a boring and mediocre historian who memorized and murmured his textbook lessons, but he was a party secretary and therefore was a bigwig in the school.[31] He had found out that she was going to church and her parents were religious. He summoned her for a private conversation in his office, asked her if it was true, and literally ordered her to stop going to church and write a statement stating that she did not share her parents' beliefs. "Or you will say goodbye to the university dreams, get it?" he barked at her, leaning over his desk. Just behind his head was a portrait of Karl Marx, and his beard jutted out from either side of the teacher's head like the fur of a colobus.[32] Nina thought it was funny, but she was too scared to laugh. She left without saying anything.

On her way home, she thought about what to do. She couldn't betray her parents. She could not declare that she didn't believe in God, either. Because she believed. Maybe she was a little angry with Him and didn't understand Him, but she believed. It seemed completely natural to her to believe. The nonsense she was taught in biology classes – about our origin of amoebas, green euglenas, ichthyosaurs, plesiosaurs and various "pithecus" – seemed

---

[31] The party secretary in every company and organization under communism is a more important figure than even the director and the chief accountant. He is often the one who orders firings and appointments of people.

[32] Black-and-white colobus is an African monkey.

absolutely ridiculous to her, and she needed a lot more faith to believe in them than in the logical idea of a Mind that had created and sustains everything.

And Nina was an honest person. Despite the lies and fantasies she invented while bewitching her classmates, she was honest with herself and her parents. No, she couldn't betray them. But what would she say to the nasty fat historian tomorrow? And more importantly, how would he react? Was he going to expose her publicly to everyone? Would she get kicked out of high school? Was he going to turn her life into hell? She was scared.

And the third unpleasant thing that weighed on her was that the New Year was coming. Basically, the New Year was a good thing. Vacation, getting up late, reading books... But she didn't want the New Year to come. Her throat was constricted by a heavy leaden foreboding that the best, the last good year of her life was coming to its end, and Nina didn't want it to end. In the new year, perhaps expulsion from school awaited her, perhaps humiliation in front of everyone. But above all, in the old year would remain the most wonderful experience, which could be never repeated. And while the year was not over yet, she felt it as a present thing. And when the new year would start, it would already belong to the past.

In the summer of this year, she fell in love. It was hopeless, of course. Too many things stood between her and him, too many years, people, and prejudices. But still, she was grateful to him for the emotions he made her feel. No one had ever told her she was beautiful before. Not for real. Not with eyes full of admiration. "Don't move, you're very beautiful like this." And she really hadn't moved because she couldn't believe her ears – for the first time in her life someone had shut her mouth. He deftly unscrewed the lens of his camera and screwed in another one, a longer one. Then he dragged back in the grass, without standing up, and began to focus the camera. She tried to lean on her other arm because the current one was numb. "Don't move!" she heard again. She froze, staring uneasily at the bulging eye of the lens. "Now turn your head to the left and look at the wall!" She carried out the order stiffened. "Excellent! Don't move!" She didn't dare move, even though her arm was completely numb now. She felt a strange warmth as she thought that on the other side of the camera he was looking at her and liking her.

Emil was not like her stupid classmates. He was a real man. And a good man, too. And he was looking at her with a man's admiration. She really wanted him to kiss her, but didn't know how to react if he actually did it. He didn't. He didn't even try. He acted like a gentleman, talked to her about photography, explained to her about colors in the light spectrum, made her speak to him in English, French, Russian, and kept laughing. No, he didn't laugh at her, but genuinely, out of joy and pride at knowing her. He kept telling her that she was amazingly beautiful; she blushed and accepted the compliment without believing it. She just wondered why he was telling her it.

A month later, he sent her a thick envelope, full of photos. And she was on every one of them. Beautiful, exquisite black and white photos, she looked like those French actresses she used to watch on the screen. Seeing them, her mother raised a terrible fuss, tore several of the pictures, and Nina burst into tears, threw herself at her, snatched them from her hands, and fled to her room. Then she hid the rest of the photos at the bottom of her schoolbag, under all her textbooks. And she checked several times a day if they were still there and that they weren't crumpled. Her mother demanded an explanation, accused her of immoral behavior, threatened her, and demanded to know who this lewd photographer was. She refused to believe that there was absolutely nothing between Nina and him, and forcibly took her to a gynecologist to make sure that her daughter was still a virgin.

Nina wrote Emil a long letter of thanks, tore it up and rewrote it several times. It seemed to her either too familiar and slobbery, or too formal and cold. She really didn't know how to write letters to a man. Anna Karenina and Natasha Rostova could not help her. They had lived too long ago, their love stories were too different from hers. She didn't dare write to him about her mother's reaction, nor admit that several photos had been destroyed. Emil answered her almost immediately, there were more photos in the letter. This time, Nina was lucky to collect the mail before her mother and hid the letter. She has been wondering all week whether she should write to Emil or not. She was afraid that if they would start a permanent correspondence, sooner or later he would have to confront her mother. And she was even more afraid that if she would stop writing to him, he would forget about her.

Finally, she decided to set a sign for herself – if he would write to her one more time, without getting a reply from her, then he really likes her and will not give her up. Then she will reply to him, and let it be what will be. He didn't write to her.

In a few days, the last sheet of the calendar, with the ugly landscape and the year 1988 in each of the four corners, would be torn off, and a new calendar with an even uglier landscape, and with 1989 written on it, would be solemnly hung in its place. Nina looked at the two eights and her eyes filled up with tears. Never, never again would the magic of eights be repeated! The next time when two eights sat next to each other on a calendar, it will be in 2088! When she will be long gone!

What was going to happen within those hundred years? Was communism really going to disappear, as her father commented with evil joy? He was so happy this year when they allowed the people to travel abroad! He was one of the first to stand in line for two nights in a row to get a red passport![33] And then he looked at it so lovingly! And he kept talking about his colleague from the Vienna Philharmonic, who arranged the documents for him to go there. Nina listened to him and couldn't believe it. She was even scared. Was her father going to leave them and never come back? Or would he take them with him? She didn't dare ask.

Would she become an actress as she dreamed of? Would she marry Emil and have children? What kind of children would they have? And would it be possible for them to go live in New Zealand, for example? Or somewhere equally far away that they could never come back and would forget about everything here?

Will there be flying cars in hundred years? Will the money disappear? Will people turn into fish? All sorts of fantasies from books she had read started wandering in her mind and tangled with one another. Her eyes continued to stare at the eights, but her tears had dried up. What exactly will matter a hundred years from now? Will her great-grandchildren be alive then? What names will they have? Where will they live? Will her country still exist, and will there be countries in the world at all? Or will the world end and the earth will be uninhabited then? Interesting or scary things await us.

---

[33] In 1988, the communist government permits ordinary citizens to travel abroad freely, for the first time. Hundreds of thousands of people flock to police passport offices to take international passports. The color of these passports is red.

Nina heard the gate to the road open and knew her brother was coming home. She had a sudden feeling that now, right now, at this moment, she had to make a very fateful choice. Now, in those few seconds before he had come in. What choice exactly? She didn't know. But she knew it would determine all her choices for the rest of her life.

At that moment the power went out. Nina reached for a match and lit a candle with a practiced gesture.

The end

"I choose, I choose... to believe!" she suddenly said out loud, the same moment her brother opened the kitchen door.

"What?" he muttered, taking off his sweaty glasses, and began to wipe them dry.

"Nothing. Hi."

"Hi. What are we having for dinner? Sauerkraut?"

"Sauerkraut."

"What did you say when I came in?"

"Nothing. I was learning a poem by heart."

"Look at this…" He took something wrapped in a newspaper out of his bag. He removed the newspaper and solemnly unfolded in front of Nina a red T-shirt on which PERESTROIKA was written in white letters. He turned it the other side like a magician. It said

GLASNOST[34] on the back.

"Where did you get it from?"

"I bought it."

"You can't wear it at school".

"I can. It's a Soviet made".

"You can't, you'll see."

"You will see what will happen."

"What?"

"At this time next year we will talk again."

"Enough rattling nonsense, go get some logs from the shed, I've put the last ones in the stove".

"Remember my words!" Her brother raised his voice while leaving. "By this time next year communism will be in the dustbin of history!"

Nina laughed and went to add rice to the sauerkraut. She checked to make sure her brother was out, and said it aloud once again, "Yes, I choose to believe!" And laughed. What to believe – she didn't know yet. Then she put the kettle on the stove so there would be hot water for the hot-water bottles when they went to bed. In all rooms of the house it was colder than in the fridge. The tiny hot-water bottles were like hot hearts in the icy sheets – the single source of joy and warmth.

---

[34] *Perestroyka* and *Glasnost* are the two slogan words of the reform process that began in the Soviet Union in the late 1980s. The words literally mean "reorganization" and "voicing."

Nina put all textbooks in her bag, attached the white collar to her uniform, looked at the two eights on the calendar again and found that the iron weights in her stomach were gone. Maybe not this year, maybe not even in ten years, but she will be what she wanted to be. She would be loved as she was. And there would be light and warmth around her. For everyone.

At that moment the power went out. Nina reached for a match and lit a candle with a practiced gesture.

To Be Continued...

The first professional orientation he received from his father: "Even the most remote village needs three persons – an innkeeper, a barber, and an undertaker. These three will never starve. Remember this lesson from me."

But Boris was an excellent student and his ambitions were bigger. He completed two master's and one doctor's degree. In Europe. He spoke three languages fluently. On top of that, he was above six feet tall, with an athletic body, and hair longer than usual; he was proud of it.

At thirty, he thought the world was almost at his feet.

Almost. Until he won Maggie. After that, the world was at his feet for real.

***

He took the glasses out of the dishwasher. Then he began to arrange them carefully on the shelf. He checked the milk in the fridge, and started the coffee machine heating up. The first customers would arrive at any moment.

He had become neither an undertaker nor a barber, but an innkeeper. More precisely, a coffeeshop-keeper.

***

The disappointments had started the moment he climbed to the top.

First, he hit a rock in his work. It took him two years to realize the sad fact that the topic of his dissertation was interesting exactly to zero people in God's world. He began to quit his ambitions one by one, and he was ready to work even as a high school teacher. And he did for five years. They were enough to almost lose his mind.

Disappointments in his personal life developed somewhat in parallel. The love line slid down. He wished Maggie had remained a dream. The materialization of the dream extinguished its light. The biggest blow was the news that she could not have children. Maggie shut herself up and got angry with the whole world – with the Lord for being so unjust; with him – for he wanted a child;

with her parents – for they had not discovered her illness on time; with the doctors – for they were so useless; with her friends – for they got pregnant and gave birth without a problem.

He was surprised to realize that, in fact, he had always wanted to be a father; to have his own continuation, to play football with his own son, to glare menacingly at his own daughter's first suitors.

He realized with bitterness that his fatherhood could easily go in the same waste basket as his doctor's and master's degrees. He started to feel like a loser. The day to break up with Maggie was unavoidable and natural. He was determined to start from the beginning once again. But it didn't work.

At the age of thirty-five, he did the craziest thing – he became a sperm donor. After a long night of quiet lonely drinking, and after a day of bitter sobering up, he decided that he didn't want his seed to go to waste. As if it was something very precious. He wished that somewhere a child of his would appear as a great fortune in the life of a lonely and desperate family; his little invisible seed would replace the sterile seed of a man who had lost hope. He felt like a dandelion with its tiny seeds blown away by the wind, and he would never see them again. But would continue to exist in them.

He researched on the Internet, and figured out what to do. They approved him very quickly. For the first and last time in his life, his diplomas and languages made a huge impression, and he was immediately approved as a donor. Asked if he had any particular birthmarks, he answered "no", and chuckled to himself. There was no way for someone to know that at twenty he had his impossible lop-ear operated on. Because of it he had let his hair grow long when he was still in high school. Most of his friends didn't even suspect that he was born with one ear like a squirrel's, and the other one perfectly stuck to his head. The idea of one day seeing child on the street, with one ear stuck to his head, and the other one stuck up, seemed amusing and exciting to him.

Then… then the turn was smooth, as if he had reached the limit of disappointments, and had stopped getting disappointed in anything. At forty-five, he remembered his father's undertaker, barber, and innkeeper, and opened a coffeeshop better than anyone else's within three neighborhoods. The employees of the four banks nearby became his regular customers, as well as most of the foreigners from the large office building across the street. Because of the languages. They enjoyed chatting in their own languages with the refined man behind the bar – he was always casually elegant, with a tempered voice and a good collection of spicy jokes. He found some joy and comfort in communicating with people, got to know so many lives, learned such incredible stories that he began seriously thinking about writing a book. He was almost happy.

✳✳✳

By three in the afternoon the coffeeshop was largely dead. Only occasional customers stopped by.

"Good afternoon."

He looked up from the book and looked at the newcomer. "Good afternoon".

Thirteen/fourteen-year-old adolescent with a stubbly mustache and a shaggy head. Not many teens came here. This one, however, was well mannered – he had said "good afternoon". The boy looked around and finally parked himself at the table by the window.

Boris went to him, smiled and asked in a friendly manner: "Would you like something?" He was always polite, even with three-year-olds.

"Uh... do you have wi-fi here?"

Boris smiled and pointed to the sticker on the window. "Of course. Would you like something to drink?"

"A coke".

He went to the bar to get the coke, and the boy added, "And some peanuts, please."

"Sure."

While putting some peanuts in a bowl, he looked at the kid. Tall, skinny, disproportionate, the boy reminded him of himself as a child. Suddenly the boy leaned back and scratched his neck. With the back of his palm! Boris nearly dropped the tray. It was the first time he ever saw someone scratch like that. Except himself. It was terribly inconvenient and inefficient. It didn't relieve the itching at all. But from a young age he did it without knowing why. And of course, he hadn't seen anyone else do it.

Boris was sitting behind the bar, sweating with tension as he struggled to think of something. Finally, he did. As he was clearing the table in the corner, an empty Fanta can *accidentally* took off and landed on the floor next to the kid. He was startled and looked up.

"Sorry!" Boris' voice was full of remorse. "I am terribly sorry! Did it hit you?"

"No, no." The young man laughed, and his face became quite childish. Then he bent down to pick up the can.

Boris watched him intently. As the boy moved, his hair fell forward, and exposed a little lop-ear. Like a squirrel's one.

Binoculars

*D*amn cats!

He kicked the greasy wrapper, tucked the bag under his arm, reached into his pocket for the keys, dropped his phone, and cursed. Naturally, it fell on the greasy wrapper. Disgusted, he picked it up with two fingers and started up the stairs. Climbing stairs is healthy. Especially when you hit your thirties.

Especially then... from today on. A stink-pot. He unlocked the door of his apartment, got in, and the greasy phone rang. F*** it! He dropped all the bags, hurried into the bathroom, tore off some toilet paper, and started scrubbing the phone. Unwittingly, he hung up. Nevermind, at least he could now clean it properly. He rummaged through the bathroom cabinet, poured disinfectant on a clear piece of paper, and thoroughly wiped the display. The phone rang again. An unknown number.

"Hello?"

"You have a packet. Can you come down?"

"Who are you?"
"Post." The voice was indifferent and full of annoyance.

Could it be that someone had remembered that he had a birthday...? Yes, of course. His father. The dear old guard. A security guard. A former reserve sergeant. He had retired early and was happy to be guarding the only bank and ATM in the town. His father loved to teach and edify him. This now had to be a book. Or another "useful" thing.

He locked the apartment, sat on the sofa and tore open the package. Hmm, it was heavy.

"Dear son, you are on the threshold of the most productive age for a man. I am proud of you. I hope you will think about other life decisions besides your career now. In 18 months my contract expires, I will have more time and I will be able to devote myself fully to a grandchild.
Happy Birthday!"

The card was written by hand, in his father's tight, disciplined script. It was a standard greetings card, with a bouquet on the front and a red "Happy Birthday" inscription. Probably the only possible option in the town's post office. He felt like laughing at the "other life decisions".

Binoculars! His father had bought him binoculars! Reflective, expensive brand, waterproof. God knows how much they cost. "Daddy's out of his mind! What should I do with binoculars in Sofia? Go hunting in South Park? Or watch the traffic police from afar?"

He rolled them in his hands, read the instruction manual, got impressed, looked through them. What to watch? The wall was four meters away. A remarkable focus, night vision, too.

He went out onto the terrace, leaned on the handrail and aimed them to the distance. Oops… he didn't expect such a clear picture. In the light of the setting sun, he suddenly saw pigeon eggshells on the roof tiles of the dilapidated house across. Wow! Even the cracks in the roof tiles were visible! He started moving the binoculars slowly and enjoying the view. It was as if he had climbed onto the roof. He aimed the binoculars down. A gutter, a back yard with flagstones and grass in between, a canvas chaise longue with a blanket and a book thrown over it... he focused better and read, "Madonna in a Fur Coat".

The plaster of the house was shelled, but the two front windows were new, even the stickers of the manufacturer were still on their frames. Why had they wasted their money? Within a year at the latest, this shack will fly away like Dorothy's cottage, and in its place will spring up a new building with apartments with small balconies, garages, and a tiny lawn at the back. And then he will be able to peer through people's windows with the binoculars...

The thought cheered him up. Just like in the movies... he will secretly observe the parallel lives of the people of the capital city. Hard workers by day, exemplary citizens who pay their mortgages... and indulge their fantasies once they're locked within the four walls of their own homes.

A bright blue. He felt that he had been watching something bright blue for several seconds. The T-shirt of the girl in the yard with the chaise longue. She was dragging a two-legged ladder. She propped it up on the roof tiles and started climbing it. He got interested and zoomed in. He could see her focused face with her tongue poking out. Her hands were white, with no trace of tanning beds. Her T-shirt was baggy, with a pink bra showing through the cut-out sleeves. This made him feel embarrassed. Where was she climbing up to like that? He looked up and saw a kitten nestled on the second row of roof tiles. Cats again!

The girl reached the edge of the roof and stretched her arm. She couldn't reach the kitten. She climbed one more step up and stretched her arm again. The kitten moved to the third row of tiles.

The girl looked down at her feet, hesitated for a moment, and then carefully stepped onto the last rung. "It's dangerous, girl! Just look at her... childish mind! She'll fall down for a stupid kitten!"

The girl flew back, along with the ladder. He jumped up, shouted, the binoculars fell from his eyes. Thank God, they had a strap. Hastily he picked them up again and frantically focused. The kitten was slowly walking down to the neighboring fence. He looked for the girl. She was lying motionless on the flagstones, the ladder was on top of her, the chaise longue had fallen to one side, and the "Madonna in a Fur Coat" was nowhere to be seen.

He stood up frightened, about to call her by shouting, but he felt it would sound stupid. Without binoculars, the view was unclear and distant. The girl on the ground looked like a discarded workman's overall. He looked up, left, right, down... no one but him had seen. He didn't hesitate anymore.

He threw the binoculars on the sofa, put the phone in his pocket, grabbed a bottle of water from the fridge, and ran out.

The girl was unconscious, there was blood around, but he couldn't tell from where exactly. She was petite, nicely rounded, with a beautiful bust under the T-shirt. But now her lips were frighteningly purple. He frantically dialed 112[35], grabbed the girl's wrist and felt for a pulse.

---

35 112 is the emergency number in Europe.

To move her? No, he had read on the Internet that such victims should not be moved to avoid further damage. God, let them come faster! They came.

He promised to lock the house and to find her documents.

*****

It was before eight o'clock. The sink was full of dishes, the carpet had to be laid after the pounding, and there were still six lessons from the questionnaire to be learned, but she needed rest, after all! Good thing, at least the Hemodialysis Center was in the next intersection, so she had only five minutes to walk. Now she would take a nap for half an hour, then she'd wash the dishes, lay the carpet, and have dinner. Then, after connecting the first patients to the machines, she will have half an hour to learn at least one lesson of the questionnaire. Then, once she arrived home around midnight, she would learn the rest. And she would have at least three hours to sleep. Great.

No, that was unbearable! Someone had to forbid these cats to produce kittens all the time and everywhere! It was meowing somewhere right above her head. A weak, crying meowing, but unceasing. A real Chinese torture! She got up, slipped on her T-shirt and went out to the back of the house. She pulled out the landlady's old ladder and dragged it in the direction of the meowing. Was it stable? She shook it with her hand, it seemed steady. She started slowly climbing up. Ugh, she hated heights!

Bang, here is the criminal! Come here, kitty-kitty... goosy, black and yellow, with wide blue eyes, the kitten meowed at regular intervals like a wind-up toy. She stretched her arm. No, it didn't work. Okay, there was one more step. She stretched her arm again. She touched the fluff, but the kitten got scared and moved further up. "F*** it! I'll kill myself because you!" She looked down, the flagstones seemed quite far away. Shit, if she left it here, it would meow for at least three days! Oh, she would hold on to the gutter with one hand. It looked secure.

***

The retired Sergeant, pensioner, and security guard of the only bank and the only ATM in the town, Krasimir Stratev, gave a satisfied inspection of the apartment. He walked slowly, with the measured step of a soldier. With his hands folded behind his back, he opened and closed the doors as if he was letting in guests. Everything was spotlessly clean, smelling of air freshener. He opened the wardrobe. The critical examination found no irregularities there, either. He entered the kitchen, counted the bottles in the refrigerator, moved the napkin-holder from the shelf to the table, wiped out invisible crumbs from it, and rocked contentedly on his toes and heels.

He saw the gray car in the parking bay, walked into the hallway, looked at himself in the mirror, smoothed the hair above his left ear with a customary gesture, moved the picture of his wife an inch to the left on the shoe-case, and waited for the doorbell with sparkling eyes.

"So, a miracle, you say?" Sergeant Stratev had leaned back in the couch, crossed one leg over the other, and stretched out his left arm on the backrest.

"Well, there is no other explanation." muttered Simmy.[36] "Such an unthinkable coincidence... what else can we call it?"

"Are you okay now? There won't be any lasting effects, right?"

"They said *no*. Well, my back hurts when I stand straight, I can't lift my left arm as much as my right, but it seems like there is nothing else."

"And the head? How come you didn't hit it?"

"Apparently, I fell on a book."

"Here you are! Reading books is a lifesaver!" Dimo[37] laughed.

"Even Agatha Christie's crime stories."

"Which Agatha Christie?"

"Madonna-In-Something... Could it be Raymond Chandler? I didn't know he has written such book."

"Ali Sabahattin," said Simmy with a mocking look in her eyes.

"Who?"

---

[36] Simmy – a pet name for Simona, a Bulgarian female name
[37] Dimo – a pet name for Dimitar, a Bulgarian male name

"Ali Sabahattin. The author of Madonna in a Fur Coat."

"Is this a pen-name?"

"No."

"A Turk has written about Madonnas?"

"Don't laugh, read it. It's a very nice book."

"Maybe some Madonna got into the harem of the sultan?"

Sergeant Stratev leaned forward energetically and topped up the glasses.

"Cheers to the miracle!"

"Cheers to your binoculars, Dad! It's as if someone had told you to send them to me! You still haven't told me how much you paid for them."

"I had a special advisor."

Dimo looked at his father with curiousity. Simmy, too. But their father said nothing, just sipped with satisfaction.

Even the pajamas of Sergeant Stratev were impeccably ironed. He moved solemnly from the bedroom to the living room, knocked, and hearing a *yes* entered, his left palm stretched forward. Simmy and Dimo looked at him simultaneously.

"These are my and your mother's wedding rings. I bought them from a truck-driver long time ago. They are a bit out of fashion, but you can have them made as you wish."

"But, Father! We have money for rings, no need!"

"I didn't say you need them. This is family gold." Dimo felt like laughing at the solemn intonation.

"Okay, Dad, thank you very much."

"Good night."

"Good night," they both answered in one voice.

Huddled on the couch, Simmy and Dimo were looking at the thick gold rings. A kind of tender sadness came over Dimo. He remembered his mother's hands – with long fingers, small nails, and fine blond hairs on the wrists. They smelled of hand cream when they covered him at bedtime. A cat had climbed up the linden tree outside, and two other cats were serenading her from below.

Damn cats!

Seargant Stratev closed the Bible, took off his glasses, placed them carefully on the nightstand, kissed the picture of his wife, folded his hands in prayer, and quietly said, "But when he was yet a great way off, his father saw him...[38] God, thank you for giving me the idea of the binoculars. I would never have thought of it." Then he lay down on his side and fell asleep immediately, like a soldier.

The serenade outside continued.

38Luke 15:20 (KJV)

НЕОБИЧАЙНИ РЕШЕНИЯ

Огромни благодарности на...

… моя съпруг и моите синове, с които се чувствам специална, защитена и винаги нащрек.

… Рамона Харпър, която вярва в мен, повече отколкото аз вярвам в себе си.

… Адам Фъргюсън, който е най-търпеливият и издържлив проджект мениджър на света.

… Енгин Акюрек, който е не само дяволски добър актьор, но и разказвач, който те подтиква да разказваш, и човек, който буди човешкото в човеците..

… и на всички непознати хора, които ме провокират да надничам в живота им.

КАК СЕ СТАВА ПИСАТЕЛ

Елена беше дълго чакано дете. Майка ѝ я роди на 42. Но се роди с дефект – дясното ѝ стъпало беше обърнато почти под прав ъгъл спрямо лявото. В далечните години на комунизма за операции в чужбина и дума не можеше да става. Българските лекари казаха, че няма смисъл да я оперират. Предписаха ѝ специални ортопедични обувки.

В училище ѝ се подиграваха, беше освободена от физическо. Никога не отиде на купон, никой никога не я покани на танц. Макар да ходеше без патерици, се клатеше вляво-вдясно, походката ѝ беше мудна и тромава.

На всичкото отгоре, в първи клас разбра, че ще трябва да носи и очила. Грозните пластмасови рамки скриха единственото, с което печелеше симпатиите на хората – миловидното ѝ лице. Обичаше книгите, четеше много и дори пишеше. Учителката ѝ по литература в гимназията я хвалеше постоянно, пишеше ѝ шестици, предричаше ѝ бъдеще на литератор, четеше откъси от есетата ѝ пред класа. Но в хормонално доминираната възраст на гимназията литературните способности бяха по-скоро повод за нови подигравки, отколкото за възхищение.

Мечтаеше да учи литература, но се страхуваше, че ако стане учителка, няма да има смелост да се изправи един ден пред учениците си. Представяше си, че подигравките ще продължат оттам, където ученическите години ги бяха прекъснали. Представяше си как куцука от вратата до бюрото при влизане в час, а отстрани се чуват хихикания.

Все пак реши да кандидатства. В деня преди изпита почина майка ѝ. После Елена трябваше да започне работа. Най-доброто, което ѝ предложиха, беше да продава вестници в една будка на кръстовището на два големи пловдивски булеварда.

После падна комунизмът. После си отиде и баща ѝ. Тя остана сама в малкия апартамент. И в будката за вестници. Смениха се няколко парламента, правителства, България стана европейска държава, по булевардите от двете ѝ страни изчезнаха ладите и трабантите, появиха се тойоти и мерцедеси. Самата будка беше купена от един бизнесмен, после от друг, после от трети. Смениха я с по-голяма, след това – с по-малка, после с жълта. По някое време Елена временно излезе в отпуска, защото ремонтираха тротоара, върху който будката се мъдреше. После посадиха дървета, те пораснаха и почнаха да хвърлят сянка върху нея. После хората почти спряха да купуват вестници.

Работното ѝ време си остана същото – сутрин в седем отключваше, изваждаше вестниците и списанията и ги подреждаше на широката лавица. Когато валеше дъжд, ги покриваше с найлон. В седем и половина идваше дистрибуторът и оставяше новите пакети. Тя си имаше миниатюрно столче, голямо брезентово портмоне за дребни, мъничко вентилаторче на батерии да я спасява в летните жеги и дебел вълнен шал от баба ѝ, сгънат под рафта отвътре, с който зимно време си завиваше краката. В три часа прибираше вестниците, заключваше и се отправяше у дома. Всеки ден без неделя.

Всеки нов собственик на будката я оставяше на работа, защото я съжаляваше, защото тя работеше съвестно и защото се задоволяваше с малка заплата.

В три и половина Елена минаваше през супермаркета, купуваше строго определени неща в строго определени дни, прибираше се вкъщи, правеше си вечеря и пишеше. Четеше и пишеше. До полунощ. После заспиваше и в шест сутринта кръговратът продължаваше.

Всяка година си правеше нови ортопедични обувки по поръчка, защото се износваха бързо. Вкъщи ходеше с пантофи, в които имаше специални стелки. Дрехи си купуваше четири пъти в годината, от едни и същи магазини. С годините някои от тях изчезваха, появяваха се нови и тя изпитваше стрес всеки път, когато се налагаше да търси нов магазин.

Приятели нямаше. Познаваше само хората от входа и то, защото те познаваха майка ѝ и баща ѝ. Но възрастните семейства си отиваха едно по едно и апартаментите се купуваха от други. Тях Елена не познаваше. Единствените, които можеха да кажат нещо за нея, бяха ортопедите и майсторите на ортопедични обувки. За всички останали тя беше една накуцваща жена на средна възраст. Никой не знаеше какви са чувствата ѝ и дали изобщо има някакви чувства.

И тя самата не знаеше. Беше любезна с клиентите на будката, познаваше почти всички по физиономия, на някои дори знаеше имената. По-приказливите споделяха с нея нещичко от живота си.

Имаше един висок сух старец, който носеше каскет зиме и лете, живееше в съседната пресечка и бабичката му беше умряла. Бивш инженер, с две деца в чужбина. Сам въртеше домакинството и не пропускаше всяка сутрин да си купи вестник. Изпитваше носталгия по комунизма.

Минаваха и две възрастни жени, които нямаха нищо общо помежду си, но толкова си приличаха, че Елена понякога ги бъркаше. И двете купуваха детски книжки за внучките си, когато им идваха на гости. От онези с картинки за оцветяване. После внучките им пораснаха, но двете баби продължиха да идват, за да си купуват кръстословици.

Имаше една Мис Судоку – засукана лелка интелектуалка, която дебнеше кога излизат сборниците с най-сложните ребуси и купуваше само тях. Дори не се интересуваше колко струват.

Минаваха и цигани да питат няма ли някой стар вестник без пари. Но Елена не можеше да раздава старите вестници, защото ги отчиташе на собственика.

По вестниците познаваше кой от коя партия е, кой кога е взел пенсия, кой се увлича по свръхестественото.

НЕОБИЧАЙНИ РЕШЕНИЯ

В началото на демокрацията трябваше да продава и еротични вестници. Ужасно се срамуваше и ги криеше под останалите, но собственикът на будката вдигна скандал, че така сваля оборота. Не смееше да погледне в очите онези, които ги купуваха. Слава Богу, по-късно забраниха продажбата им на открито и тя си отдъхна.

През декември идваха календарите за следващата година и тогава търговията се оживяваше. По едно време продаваше и поздравителни картички, но вече никой не ги купуваше.

Млади клиенти нямаше.

С някои разменяше по две-три думи, други само подаваха парите, вземаха си вестниците и тръгваха, без дори да я погледнат.

Отпуска ползваше веднъж в годината по една седмица. Но се чудеше какво да прави през нея. Обикновено спеше до късно. Нито веднъж не излезе извън Пловдив.

Всичко, което събираше в главата и сърцето си, Елена изливаше на хартия. Когато започна, пишеше на ръка. Имаше стотици изписани тетрадки, събрани в кашони от кроасани. По-късно реши да си купи компютър. Просто влезе в магазин за компютри и каза, че иска един. Младото момче в магазина я попита какъв точно и тя замълча.

- За какво ще го използвате?
- За да пиша.

Първият ѝ лаптоп и първото ѝ включване в интернет бяха най-вълнуващото нещо през целия ѝ живот. Започна да си ляга все по-късно, защото се залисваше да чете и в интернет. Всичко написано съхраняваше в спретнато подредени папки в лаптопа. Разкази, есета, новели, дори два романа.

Когато разбра, че няма да учи в университета, започна да ходи в Националната библиотека и системно да чете учебници по литература. Седеше на малкото си столче в будката (или до нея, ако беше прекалено горещо), четеше старателно и си водеше записки. После гледаше хората, които минаваха по тротоара; шофьорите на колите, които спираха на пешеходната пътека; клиентите си, които бавно се подменяха с други през годините, и ги описваше.

Нисичка тийнейджърка с тротинетка бавеше крачка, забила нос в телефона и с близалка в уста, която вадеше разсеяно и я размахваше в такт с невидимата музика в слушалките си... вечер тя се превръщаше в таен агент, който дава кодирани сигнали на колегите си чрез размахване на близалка във въздуха...

Самодоволен дебел шофьор на скъпо БМВ, който профучаваше през пешеходната пътека без да спре, вечер оживяваше като зъл хипопотам в басня...

Прегърбена старица с насълзени очи, стиснала кофичка кисело мляко, се превръщаше във фея-кръстница, която проверява добротата на хората...

Весела компания подпийнали американски туристи с шарени ризи спасяваха куче с три крака и го вкарваха тайно в самолета...

Деца с ученически раници на гърба сдобряваха скарани съседи...

Клошари, просещи пари за цигари, ставаха данъчни инспектори под прикритие...

Малкият мрачен апартамент с овехтели мебели от соца се изпълваше с хора, образи, гласове и случки. Елена така се изтощаваше да преживява и описва техния живот, че не ѝ оставаха много сили за живота навън. Ходеше равнодушно и унило по ежедневния си маршрут до будката, след това до супермаркета, казваше „добро утро" на клиентите с равен глас, местеше столчето си в жегата на деня според сянката на дърветата и дори не изпитваше глад.

Всички я мислеха за скучна и необщителна жена, лишена от интелект и въображение.

Нямаше никакви роднини, освен някакви далечни братовчеди по бащина линия. Беше ги видяла за последно на погребението на баща си. Не ѝ липсваха. Имаше си своите герои, минувачите по булевардите, градските шумове, автобуси и лястовици. Говореше предимно със себе си и с героите си. Внимаваше да не се разприказва с някой от тях, докато е на работа. Да не я помислят за луда. Но щом вечер се прибереше вкъщи, започваше да говори – на себе си; на героите в книгите, които беше чела през деня; на героите в историите, които пишеше в момента. Изприказваше целия си дневен запас от думи за два часа и притихваше, за да пише. Описваше в дневник деня, какъвто е трябвало да бъде.

Преживя цялата световна история, седнала на столчето си във или до будката – падането на комунизма, хиперинфлацията, 11 септември, влизането на България в Европейския съюз, смяната на шест правителства, ковид епидемията, украинската война... Четеше вестници, гледаше новини, но сякаш истински я интересуваше само едно – как този грозен свят да емигрира в историите ѝ, да се подчини на въображението ѝ и да стане такъв, какъвто тя го иска. Нито веднъж не излезе извън Пловдив. Но пропътува целия свят в интернет, по телевизията и в книгите. И го описа, както го видя.

Един ден започна да кашля. И не спря четири месеца. Първо помисли, че е грип, после ковид. Накрая разбра, че е нещо друго. Трийсетгодишното вдишване на автомобилни газове на едно от най-оживените кръстовища в града даде плод – рак. Тя, която не беше изпушила и една цигара в живота си, имаше рак на белите дробове. И на двата. С разсейки.

Писа до последно, дори в болницата – с маска на лицето. Накрая пак се беше върнала към писането на ръка. Сестрите я гледаха съчувствено, защото драсканиците в бележника ѝ бяха абсолютно нечетливи. Но разбираха, че това я успокоява. Помага ѝ да търпи болките.

На погребението ѝ нямаше нито един човек. Погреба я общината. На другия ден далечните братовчеди обявиха апартамента за продан, без дори да се появят. Купувачът намери кашони с тетрадки и помисли, че бившата собственичка е била учителка. От любопитство зачете една от тях.

И стана известен писател. Издаде над двайсет книги, превеждаха го в чужбина, направиха филм по две от тях. Даваше пространни интервюта, в които обясняваше как образованието му по психология му е помогнало да вижда света през женските очи. Наричаха го „невероятен“, „първият мъж, разбрал жените“.

Елена продължи да живее в своите дракони, шпиони, учителки, сервитьори, плажове, полицаи, хипопотами и феи. Макар и под друго име.

ШОПИНГ

Всичко беше заради нея. Тъпата стара крава. Надута и самодоволна, злорада докрай. Остави го на поправителен, провали му дипломирането.

Е, ако имаше баща...

Ако имаше, ама нямаше. И затова тя безнаказано си го изкара на него. Бащата на Симо го защити, всички видяха как се беше надвесил над Тачева в дъното на коридора, как ѝ говореше тихо със стиснати юмруци. И как после Симо се дипломира. А него остави на поправителен. Гледаше го със стиснати устни, с някакво стаено отмъщение в погледа: „Съжалявам, Борис. Предупредих те още миналата година, че ако продължаваш така, няма да се дипломираш“. После бавно написа красива двойка.

НЕОБИЧАЙНИ РЕШЕНИЯ

Добре де, не беше светило по литература. Но поне една тройка можеше да му пише. Само че трябваше да си го изкара на някого за унижението от бащата на Симо.

После трябваше да работи. Как се намира работа в градче с петнайсет хиляди жители? В което майка ти е една от петте фризьорки – най-опитната, но и най-възрастната? И изкарва толкова, колкото да си плащате тока и сметките? И ходи до София да купува дрехи от магазините за втора употреба, за да не разберат клиентите ѝ?

Повъртя се, поразпита тук-там... трябваше да реши – или се местят да живеят в столицата, или хваща чужбината. Майка му решително отказа местене в София – „Не мога да трупам клиентела наново. Не и в София. Няма да свикна с мръсотията и шума. Ще се разболея.“

И той започна да разглежда обявите за работа в чужбина.
За пръв път се возеше на самолет, внимаваше да не се издаде. Срам го беше, че досега не го е правил. Внимателно проследи съседа си по място как закопчава колана, после без да бърза, опипа своя и го закопча от първия път. Облегна се доволно и се загледа през стъклото.

Пилотът съобщи, че започват снижаване над Амстердам, усети вибрации и леко неприятно чувство в стомаха. Господи, какъв огромен и блестящ град! Амстердам не беше по-голям от София, но му се стори сто пъти по-светъл. А летището... цялото софийско летище можеше да се събере в един гейт на амстердамското. Заля го вълна от съвършено чужд стържещ език и той почувства паника. Английският му беше средна работа, можеше да се разбере само за обикновени неща. Добре че хората бяха толкова мили и внимателни.

Втора седмица... втора седмица навърташе по няколко километра на ден из безкрайните складове на фирмата. Единственото, което успя да запомни на нидерландски, беше „гоеде даг" и „фаарвел"[1]. Сутрин почваше в седем, вечер свършваше в седем. Сам пожела да работи извънредни часове; и без това нямаше какво да прави вечер. Повечето му колеги бяха поляци и румънци, той беше единствен българин. Градчето беше малко, вечер в шест улиците опустяваха. Почна да учи нидерландски по интернет, но вечер беше изморен, та не му спореше много.

Работата му беше да обикаля складовете и да сваля от рафтовете стоки със съответни кодове. Фирмата беше голяма, международна, май китайска, защото стоките им бяха почти сто процента китайски. Фирма за интернет търговия. Хора от цял свят купуваха по интернет и тук им опаковаха поръчките. Той беше този, който внимаваше номерът на поръчката и номерът на стоката да съвпадат. Ако се случеха рекламации за сгрешена пратка, шефовете им удържаха от надницата разходите за повторното изпращане. Затова трябваше дяволски да внимава.

Свят му се зави, като разбра колко народ пазарува по интернет. Всичко. От мехлем против гъбички до електрически косачки; от бански до газови пистолети. Понякога, освен да сверява номерата на поръчките, хвърляше по едно око и на адресите. Цяла Европа, арабските страни, Русия, Северна Африка, Южна Америка, Щатите... абе, буквално цял свят!

Развълнува се, когато за пръв път видя българско име и български адрес.

Някакъв мъж от Айтос беше поръчал семена за орхидеи. Усмихна се. Беше му приятно, че това, което той лично свали от рафта и сложи в сивия найлонов плик, ще пристигне след два дни в Айтос и някакъв неизвестен нему Атанас ще посади семенцата в саксии и ще чака да поникнат.

Стана му навик да проверява адресите и да обръща специално внимание на българските. Не бяха много. Българите купуваха предимно дрехи, козметика, разни кухненски джаджи. Повечето бяха жени. Обичаше да си представя как изглеждат тези хора, къщите им, семействата им. Понякога оглеждаше какво са поръчали и си съставяше мнение за възможностите, вкусовете им, начина им на живот. Беше някакво разнообразие в монотонното ежедневие – цял ден работа, след това малко чистене и готвене, и след това интернет на телефона. Телевизия не гледаше, така и така нищо не разбираше. Със съквартирантите не общуваше – повечето бяха пияндета и налитаха на бой. А той искаше да стои далеч от неприятности.

Понякога го задушаваше носталгията, говореше с майка си, разстройваше се, когато усети, че тя едва се сдържа да не заплаче. Мечтаеше да седне на любимото си място в кафенето зад автогарата, веселата леля Пепа да му донесе кафе, да му изтърси клюките от града и да му се оплаче от болестите и от дъщеря си – всичко в рамките на трийсет секунди. Не можеше да понася холандските домати и блудкави супи. Ядеше му се истинска храна. Тиха ярост клокочеше в гърдите му всеки път, когато се сетеше за тъпата крава Тачева. Заради нея е тук! Заради гадната ѝ дребна злобна душица! Фантазираше как изкарва достатъчно пари да плати на две яки момчета да я спукат от бой, а тя да не знае откъде ѝ е дошло.

Беше обикновен петък, в петък не се случваха такива работи. В петък всичко ставаше бързо, защото идваха почивни дни и никой не се мотаеше, не искаше да рискува да му натресат допълнителна работа през уикенда. Но ето че се случи! Видя на плика „Bulgaria“, по навик прочете името и адреса. Премига два пъти, обърна плика към светлината и пак прочете. „Светослава Тачева, ул. „Архангел Михаил“, 29...“ И неговият град! Приседна на количката, изпита внезапна нужда да пийне вода. Тъпата крава пазаруваше по интернет! Никога не беше си го представял. И изобщо, досега адрес от неговия град не беше се появявал. Там всичко бе толкова забавено, заспало, замръзнало, че понякога му се струваше, че дори няма интернет.

А дъртата злобна Тачева да рови по сайтове и да пазарува с карта... беше равно на фантастика.

Но адресът и името бяха изписани ясно. Зачете се в поръчката, погледна номера... беше рокля. Официална безвкусна евтина китайска рокля от изкуствена материя. За двайсет и три евро и трийсет и пет цента. Намалена два пъти. Сигурно беше канена на някоя сватба и беше решила да се издокара. Кой знае как щеше да лъже, че я е купила от София, от някой бутик. Злобата го заля както никога досега. Тази тъпа и грозна рокля, която държеше в ръцете си, опакована в просташки найлон, щеше да се опъне по противния ѝ задник и провисналите ѝ тлъсти ръце. Прииска му се да омагьоса роклята, та като я облече онази, изведнъж да се подпали и да я изгори жива. Нямаше начин да не изпълни поръчката. Е, можеше да сложи три номера по-малка рокля, но така само щеше да забави нещата, пък и щяха да го глобят. Знаеше се точно коя поръчка от кого на коя дата е заредена.

Продължи машинално да обикаля рафтовете, да сверява номерата и да пълни пликовете. Планът се оформи много бързо. Вече знаеше къде са разположени камерите и какво хващат – това беше едно от първите неща, в които го посветиха поляците. Имаше „мъртви точки“, където те се криеха да пият в работно време. Застана така, че да е с гръб към камерата и сръчно мушна плика с роклята в гащеризона си. Продължи да обикаля, докато стигна тоалетната. Без да бърза, слезе от количката и с нехайна походка се запъти към вратата. Влезе и се заключи. Тук камери нямаше. Отвори плика и разгледа противната рокля. После обилно и с наслада се изпика върху нея. После се изсекна и размаза сополите от вътрешната страна на яката.

Изсуши я на сешоара за ръце. Материята беше изкуствена и изсъхна за нула време. Подуши я, миришеше противно. Сгъна я и я пъхна обратно в плика. Дано мръсницата я облече така, без да я пере.

НЕОБИЧАЙНИ РЕШЕНИЯ

През следващите два дни беше в изключително настроение. Научи падежите на нидерландския и разликата между de и het[2], справяше се толкова добре, че дори шефът го похвали.

Светослава Тачева плати на куриера и нетърпеливо разкъса сивия найлонов плик. Роклята не беше същата като на снимката в сайта. Отблизо видя колко евтина е материята, но отдалеч изглеждаше добре. Сигурно ще я хареса.

Само преди една година не беше и мислила, че с Ленчето ще станат приятелки. Все пак Ленчето беше най-обикновена фризьорка, а тя имаше филология! Пък и синът ѝ беше от мързеливите. Учеше, колкото да не заспи, но с претенции. Точно покрай него се запознаха. Ленчето идва при нея да я моли да не къса Борис, да не му пречи да се дипломира. Отказа ѝ, стига е давала шанс на идиоти и мързеливци! Стига ѝ срамът със Симо, за който целият град говореше. Но какво да прави, като баща му открито я заплаши. Сума ти време я беше страх да се прибира по тъмно заради него. Но Ленчето не беше опасна. Възпитана жена беше, наистина, дожаля ѝ за нея, но... Срещна я случайно в супермаркета два дни, след като Борис беше заминал за Холандия. Разговориха се, опита да я успокои, че това е за негово добро, че така ще стане отговорен, ще се научи да се организира и да работи. Ленчето се съгласяваше машинално, но тъгата не изчезна от очите ѝ.

Покани я на кафе. След три дни повториха, в неделя пак. Оказа се, че имат много общи неща, започнаха да си ходят на гости и да гледат филми заедно.

Тя редовно я питаше за Борис и му пращаше поздрави. Предполагаше, че Ленчето никога не му ги предава.

Беше ѝ казала направо, че Борис я мрази и обвинява нея за несполуките си. На Тачева съвестта ѝ беше чиста, но все пак искаше да се реваншира. Когато веднъж Ленчето с въздишка сподели как ще преправя рокля на сестра си, за да се издокара за сватба на роднини, Тачева взе решение. Какво толкова! И без това не беше правила подаръци на никого от години. Разгледа няколко сайта, избра една ефектна, но намалена рокля и я поръча.

Борис дълго се взира в снимката на телефона си, мислеше, че е някаква зрителна измама. Майка му държеше чаша, прическата ѝ беше красива. „Привет. Тук съм на сватбата на братовчедка ти Тони. Много съжаляваха, че теб те няма. Целувам те!"

---

[1] Goede dag – добър ден, vaarwel – довиждане на нидерландски.

[2] De – обща форма за мъжки и женски род в нидерландския, het – форма за среден род.

СТРАХ

Дорина се огледа за сто и първи път. Загаси лампата. После пак я светна. Завъртя се, за да се види в гръб.

Трябваше да му откаже! Да измисли нещо, да отложи...
Но нали и тя го иска?...
Не, това ще е краят...
Как така краят? Ако я обича, значи я обича...

Тази синкава паяжина капиляри около глезените! Толкова е грозна!...
Е, поне ръцете ѝ са красиви – с бледа кожа и ален маникюр...
Но с кафяви петна...
Най-важно е да не позволи да ѝ свали сутиена! Или да го свали на тъмно. Боже, какъв бюст имаше някога...

НЕОБИЧАЙНИ РЕШЕНИЯ

Само че „някога“ тя лекомислено подари сочния си бюст, стройните крака, нежната кожа и всичко останало на Тони. На идиота и пияницата Тони. И сега за Анди бяха останали трохи.

Тони е отдавна изхвърлен, децата им отдавна поеха по широкия свят, тя отдавна не работи като ненормална по дванайсет часа на ден седем дни в седмицата, за да оцелее. Цялата си пролет и цялото си лято изживя с гордо стиснати устни, сама, стегната като навита пружина. След горчивия Тони, след кошмарните десет години брак на побои, пиене, скандали и мизерия реши да зачеркне мъжете от живота си. Ще се оправя сама! И се оправи. Отгледа децата сама, създаде бизнес сама. Сега имаше салон за красота и четири момичета работеха за нея. И есента чукаше на вратата ѝ.

Първоначално не разбра, че Андрей е Той. Случайна среща в случайно кафене. Естествен, с оригинално чувство за хумор, прошарен, понатежал, със силни пръсти. Много приятен мъж. Разговорите с него бяха сладки, винаги си тръгваше от тях някак лека, весела, спокойна.

Постепенно и ненатрапчиво той почна да се грижи за нея – сервиз за колата ѝ, дребни ремонти вкъщи, интересни представления, пикници-изненади. Последните спомени за подобна грижа бяха потънали назад в мрака на миналото. Много назад, в детството. А мъжът беше баща ѝ.

Андрей не правеше намеци за секс. Това я успокояваше и притесняваше едновременно.

Защото усети, че се влюбва. Уплаши се не на шега. Нарочно увеличи дистанцията, опита се да го гледа с чужди очи. Надяваше се всеки миг да открие в него нещо от Тони, за да може с облекчение и огорчение да каже: „Не, няма смисъл“. Но Анди неизменно я гледаше с весели искрени очи. Топлината му я обгръщаше като одеяло, беше ѝ уютно и спокойно.

И той беше страдал, разбира се. Но не се къпеше в страданието си, не го вееше като знаме и не чакаше съчувствие. „Никой не ми е виновен“ – казваше.

Макар да харесваха различни филми, обичаха да ходят на кино заедно, защото после прекарваха още два-три приятни часа в спорове за филма. За пръв път я докосна в киното. Просто преметна ръка през рамото ѝ, наведе се към нея и докосна с устни ухото ѝ. „Много хубав парфюм“ – каза. Всички емоции, които беше изпитвала като ученичка, се побраха в десет секунди. Стана ѝ горещо, оглуша за няколко мига, понечи да се притисне към него, но най-вече се уплаши.

След филма седнаха на по питие.

- Не те притискам. Но много искам – ѝ каза по-късно, наведен през масата и хванал ръката ѝ. – Знаеш, че те обичам. Казвал съм ти го много пъти.

- Знам – гърлото ѝ беше сухо като страница от книга. – Не мислѝ, че аз не искам.

- Добре, ти решаваш.

Минаха няколко месеца. Срещаха се редовно, той дори остави свои пантофи и дрехи в апартамента ѝ; дори понякога преспиваше там. На дивана в хола.

- Някакъв проблем ли има? – беше я прегърнал отзад през кръста, заровил устни в косата ѝ. Тя миеше зеленчуци на мивката.

- Не, защо?

Той залепи дълга целувка на врата ѝ, спусна бавно ръце надолу, очерта формите ѝ и се отдръпна. Дорина продължи да мие зеленчуци. Търкаше ги старателно и мълчеше.

Да, беше глупаво. Но как да му каже, че се страхува? Облечена, изглеждаше страхотно. Всички приятелки ѝ завиждаха за стройната фигура. Но как да остане пред него гола и беззащитна? Болезненият спомен за пияния Тони, който ѝ крещи: „Виж се на к'во приличаш! Махай тоя увиснал задник от очите ми!", не беше се стопил напълно. Не, Анди не е такъв, никога няма да я обиди. Но самата мисъл да предизвика отвращение в очите му, беше непоносима. Защо не го срещна, когато беше на двайсет!...

Бавно избърса ръце, пое въздух и се обърна. Подпря се на мивката и го погледна в очите.

- Добре, прав си. Държа се глупаво – и пак преглътна.
- Не се напрягай. Просто ме палиш, като си наоколо и едва се сдържам.
- Чак пък да те паля... – засмя се смутено и наведе очи.
- Да, много – каза бавно, почти шепнешком.
- Хайде, бягай сега да не закъснееш. Ще те чакам довечера – и го прегърна силно. Той я притисна.

Е, вече е довечера. Следобед беше на козметик и маникюр. Чувстваше се като ученичка преди първа среща – беше ѝ смешно, срамуваше се, но най-вече се страхуваше. Как бяха стъпките на този танц, по дяволите? Не помнеше.

Огледа се за сто и първи път. Загаси лампата. После пак я светна. Завъртя се, за да се види в гръб.

Беше жалка! Скъпото копринено бельо не скриваше нищо. Само откриваше. Луничаво деколте, плисета по шията, стрии по корема, бричове и тези ужасни, ужасни сини капиляри! Навсякъде по краката ѝ! Взе фондьотена и почна да го втрива яростно в бедрата си. Доплака ѝ се. Дишай, дишай дълбоко! Преглътни! Още веднъж... точно така! Няма да се гримираш пак я!

Нали го искаше? Боже, колко го искаше! Кожата ѝ, душата ѝ се гърчеха за малко нежност. Дългогодишното въздържание не беше изкоренило болката. Нито желанието.

Зави се плътно с халата и отиде да отвори.

Отпусна се небрежно върху ръката му. Внимателно покри гърдите си с чаршафа. Отдолу косъмчетата по кожата му я гъделичкаха. Обърна се надясно, орловият му нос изглеждаше черен на фона на лунната светлина. Той лежеше по гръб с ръце под главата, с отворени очи и гледаше усмихнат тавана. Тя понечи да го попита за какво мисли, но си спомни вица за мухата и се засмя вътрешно. После намести удобно глава под рамото му и затвори очи. Боже, как хубаво миришеше!

СТОПАДЖИЙКАТА

Ники беше в страхотно настроение. Новата му кола мъркаше като коте, от утре започваше отпуската и той току-що беше хапнал от любимите си сандвичи на бензиностанцията. Чашката с кафето се полюшваше леко в поставката си, радиото свиреше евъргрийни, от климатика духаше свеж въздух. Ники не усети как е почнал да си свирка с уста в такт с музиката.

До табелата на отклонението едно момиче беше седнало върху куфар и уморено махаше на минаващите коли. Не, не беше от „контингента". По-скоро симпатична студентка, която явно се прибираше вкъщи за ваканцията. Ники натисна спирачките и отби. После даде назад към момичето. Тя се оживи, стана бързо и грабна куфара си.
- Закъде сте?

НЕОБИЧАЙНИ РЕШЕНИЯ

- За Смолян. Вие закъде пътувате?

- Точно за там! Качвайте се.

Ники хвърляше от време на време по някой поглед към спътничката си. Никакъв страх ли нямаха тези момичета? Или не им пукаше? Опита се да я заговори, тя отговаряше едносрично, а след десетина минути заспа. Главата ѝ почна да се люшка насам натам, докато той въртеше по завоите. Ники изпита леко разочарование. Искаше му се да води лек, приятен разговор, дори да пофлиртува невинно с хубавицата. Очакваше целият свят да споделя приповдигнатото му настроение.

След Пампорово момичето изведнъж отвори очи.
- Спрете бързо, моля ви. Лошо ми е.

Ники сръчно отби вдясно и пусна аварийните светлини. Дискретно гледаше напред, после започна да си рови в телефона, докато тя повръщаше в канавката край пътя. Да, случва се почти на всеки, който не е свикнал със завоите. Ники се подсмихна вътрешно. На него никога не му се случваше.

Момичето се върна в колата, отпусна се уморено на седалката и се извини.
- Моля ви, няма нищо. Нормално е. Сега по-добре ли сте?

- Да, благодаря. Аз затова исках да спя, докато пътуваме, за да не ми стане лошо, но...
- Спокойно, почти стигнахме. Ще карам по-бавно.

Малко преди Смолян момичето пребледня и каза, че пак му е лошо. Ники отби, тя слезе и отново повърна в канавката. Когато се върна, изглеждаше изтощена и все още много бледа.
- Ако не ви е добре, да карам направо в болницата, а?
- Не, няма нужда – гласът на момичето беше почти шепот.

В този момент затвори очи и припадна. Изсули се надолу в седалката и Ники се уплаши не на шега. Изтича от другата страна на колата, отвори вратата и я привдигна да седне. Плесна я лекичко по бузите, но тя не реагира.
- Момиче, ей, момиче! – в паниката не успя да си спомни името ѝ, макар тя да се беше представила, когато се качи.

Плесна я още няколко пъти, този път по-силно, бузите ѝ леко порозовяха. Той видя, че диша и се поуспокои. Ама че работа! Навлече си беля с това момиче. Сега не може да я зареже на първата бензиностанция в града. Реши да я закара в болницата.

В Бърза помощ бяха отегчени и експедитивни. Ники притеснено чакаше в приемната, докато вътре ѝ правеха изследвания. Някак не беше прилично да си тръгне и да я зареже. Трябваше да разбере какво ѝ е и ако има нужда, да направи нещо за нея. Реши да не се обажда на Таня, за да не я притеснява излишно. Пък и Таня си беше ревнивичка. Щеше да почне един безкраен разпит коя е тази, защо е с него, колко време са пътували заедно и прочие. Нямаше да му повярва, че просто се беше поддал на импулса на доброто си настроение и в изблик на великодушие беше решил да помогне на бедното момиче.

- Вие ли докарахте Марияна Янакиева? Може да влезете да я видите.

Ники стреснато погледна нагоре. До него се беше изправила администраторка от болницата.
- Да, благодаря – и се изправи. – Къде е?
- В трета стая. Честито.

Ники тръгна машинално към трета стая, без да регистрира и обработи последната дума на администраторката. Влезе и видя момичето да седи в леглото с включена система в лявата ръка.
- Честито, приятелката ви е бременна – усмихна се младият лекар, който попълваше документите на Марияна.
- Какво?

- Прилошаването е съвсем нормално, още повече сте пътували по завои. Нека да ѝ изтече системата и може да си я вземете вкъщи. И никакъв стрес, никакво натоварване!
- Ама чакайте, имате грешка. Аз не познавам това момиче. Просто я качих на стоп. В колата ѝ прилоша и я докарах тук.

Младият лекар погледна Ники изненадано. След това стрелна момичето въпросително.
- Недей така – Марияна почти шепнеше, навела надолу очи, изчервена. – Много гаден начин да се отървеш от мене. Сега не е моментът!

Ники не повярва на ушите си.
- Ти луда ли си? – После се обърна към доктора – Докторе, не знам какви ги говори тая! Даже името ѝ не помнех, докато не ми го каза администраторката! – После пак се нахвърли на момичето – Виж какво, не знам каква игра играеш, но номерът ти е гаден и няма да мине!

Момичето не отговори, само избухна в сълзи. Докторът изгледа Ники враждебно.
- Не я познавам изобщо, не разбирате ли! – Ники извиси глас, почти крещеше. – Хубаво ми казваше баща ми едно време, че никое добро не остава ненаказано! Качих я на стоп малко след Пловдив, седеше си върху куфара до една табела и я съжалих!

НЕОБИЧАЙНИ РЕШЕНИЯ

- Добре, господине, спокойно. Има достатъчно начини да докажете, че не сте бащата на детето ѝ.

- Да доказвам ли? Тя да докаже фантасмагориите си! Боже, какво ми дойде до главата... – и Ники излезе разгневен от стаята, като тресна вратата зад гърба си.

Когато се прибра вкъщи, от приповдигнатото му настроение не беше останала и следа. Само да не стигне до ушите на Таня! Че Смолян беше малък град. Каквато беше ревнива, щеше да го изпепели само с приказки.

Но на другия ден заминаха на ваканция в Гърция и идиотската случка избледня в съзнанието му.

Младият лекар в Спешното беше дискретен, но дежурната сестра не беше. Скучаеща, любопитна и бъбрива стара мома, за която единствената истинска наслада бяха пикантните тайни на другите. А когато не можеше да научи нови, си ги съчиняваше. Историята с бременната стопаджийка беше мълниеносно украсена и преразказана десетина пъти на колеги и пациенти.

Когато след седмица Ники, Таня и трите им деца се върнаха от Гърция, ги очакваше неприятен сюрприз. Малкият задремал в лятната жега Смолян изглеждаше видимо развеселен от пикантната история. За Ники настанаха тежки дни. Малко е да се каже, че Таня му вдигна скандал. „Скандал“ беше твърде скучна и благовъзпитана дума, за да опише неконтролируемия поток от лава, изливащ се върху бедната му глава от всички страни.

Тя демонстративно събра три куфара багаж и замина заедно с трите деца при майка си в съседния квартал. Ники стисна зъби и реши просто да изчака да ѝ мине. Обикновено ставаше за два-три дни. Но този път нещата се развиваха все по-зле. Таня не спираше да говори. С майка си, със сестра си, с колежките си, с фризьорката си, с работниците на бензиностанциите и касиерките в супермаркетите. Описваше Ники като похотлив сатир със святкащи очи и капещи от устата лиги.
- И ти не си в безопасност! – приключваше обикновено тирадата си пред поредната съседка. – Нищо че си минала шейсетте. Моят изрод е способен на всичко, казвам ти!

Нещата излязоха извън контрол. Таня не даваше на децата да го виждат, „за да не им направи нещо, че са момичета“. Обаждаше се на приятелите и колегите му да ги разпитва къде ходи, какво прави и най-вече „с коя мръсница“. Каза да му предадат да си наеме адвокат, защото тя ще заведе дело за развод. Ники се видя в чудо. Приятелите му познаваха Таня и му вярваха, че е невинен, но шефовете в службата взеха да го гледат лошо. За нещастие, прекият му началник беше жена и той усети рязка промяна в отношението към себе си. Опита се да поговори с нея, но тя го изгледа студено:

- Не очаквах това от вас, Раев. Има си граници, които не бива да се прекрачват.

- Никакви граници не съм прекрачил – опита да се защити Ники. – Всичко това са приказки, които разпространява ревнивата ми жена.

Въпреки това не му повярваха. Стефан, най-добрият му приятел, го посъветва да си направи ДНК тест.

- Така ще сложиш край на цялата сага – каза му той.

- Съмнявам се.

- Е, като види Таня черно на бяло, че бебето на онази не е от теб, ще клекне. Няма да има избор.

Ники мисли, мисли и накрая реши да го направи. Щеше да му коства доста разправии, но в крайна сметка, в момента беше на косъм да си загуби семейството заради една идиотка! Отиде в Бърза помощ, обясни какво иска и оттам му съдействаха много охотно. Нали целият персонал на Спешното беше в течение на вълнуващата сага, започнала в тяхното отделение. Между лекарите и сестрите дори започнаха да текат облози дали накрая детето ще се окаже негово, или не.

- Няма как да е негово. Ако беше, щеше ли сам да поиска ДНК тест?...

- Ама той решил да се разведе и да се ожени за момичето, не чухте ли? Затова иска тест, за да признае официално бебето...
- Хм... той е доста заможен. Като нищо ще плати където трябва да му издадат какъвто си поиска ДНК тест...
- Глупости. Ще има тройна експертиза...

Ники се опита да издири злощастната стопаджийка, но безуспешно. Оказа се, че постоянният ѝ адрес е в Плевен, нямаше нищо общо със Смолян. Ники отиде дори до Плевен, но никой не беше чувал за нея на посочения адрес. Стори му се нелепо да се разхожда с нейна снимка и да пита хората дали са я виждали. Пък и нямаше нейна снимка. Тогава ще – не ще се обърна към полицията. Обясни какъв е случаят и те я намериха.

Ники се срещна с нея в кафенето на една бензиностанция близо до София. Изглеждаше наедряла, бременността вече ѝ личеше.
- Защо ми извъртя този номер? – попита я студено той.

Нямаше как да избегне срещата, защото беше получила призовка от съда. Гледаше го смутено и упорито.
- Бях отчаяна.
- Сега, обаче, аз съм отчаян – злобно отвърна той. – Знаеш ли какви беди ми докара до главата! Знаеш ли, че жена ми ме напусна и иска развод? Знаеш ли, че не съм виждал децата си

повече от месец! Знаеш ли, че шефовете вече ме смятат за неблагонадежден!

- Съжалявам – Марияна го погледна право в очите, но в тях нямаше кой знае какво съжаление. – Не съм го направила, за да ти докарам беди. Просто исках някой да ми помогне.

- Ами да беше ми казала! Щях да ти помогна!

- Сега ще ми помогнеш ли?

- Не ти липсва нахалство, обаче.

- Виж, няма да те занимавам с тъжната история на живота си и да ти изброявам глупостите, които съм направила. Просто моля за помощ. Аз ще направя ДНК теста, за да си оправиш бъркотията в живота, а ти ми дай малко пари да си наема жилище за една година.

- Слушай, ти ДНК теста ще го направиш, защото те задължава съдът! Що за наглост да ми искаш пари! Аз трябва да те съдя и да искам пари за нанесени морални вреди!

- Добре, бе. Знам, че ти си прав и съвършен, а аз съм тъпа кучка, която е спала с кой знае кого – тъмните ѝ очи го гледаха упорито, ъгълчетата им бяха пълни със сълзи. – Просто те моля! Прояви човещина.

На Ники не му се спореше. А и дълбоко в душата му стана жал за нея. Бедната малка тъпачка. Не ѝ обеща нищо, само се уговориха за теста. За всеки случай той поиска двоен тест, макар кръвният да беше достатъчен.

Мина един месец, докато резултатите излязат. През това време Ники няколко пъти опита да се сдобри с Таня, но без резултат. Не ѝ каза, че е направил ДНК тест. Искаше да ѝ го навре в лицето, да ѝ вдигне контра-скандал на отмъщението. Репетираше думите, с които ще я принуди да му се извини и дори предвкусваше смирението ѝ през следващите месеци.

Накрая тестът пристигна. С пресъхнала уста Ники отвори плика. Не че очакваше бебето да е негово. Просто предстоеше да сложи точка на една дълга агония. Две страници, пълни с непонятни медицински термини, таблици и думи на латински. Най-важното се мъдреше най-отдолу: „Плодът в 24-та гестална седмица на Марияна Янакиева има 100% несъвпадение с генетичния материал от Николай Раев". Йес! Внимателно сгъна листа отново по същите гънки, пъхна го в плика и с клокочещо ликуване в гърдите извади телефона от джоба си. После се спря. Не, няма да се обажда на Таня. Просто ще даде изследването на адвоката си, той да го връчи на нейния адвокат. Само дето ужасно му се искаше да зърне отнякъде лицето ѝ, докато го чете.

После забеляза, че в плика има и втори лист. Отвори и го зачете разсеяно. Още неразбираеми латински заклинания. „... жизнеспособни сперматозоиди – 0. Заключение: Пълен и необратим стерилитет. Причини: неизяснени".

Ники прочете няколко пъти листа, обърна го от другата страна, но там не пишеше нищо повече. Прочете най-отгоре, видя името си, дори ЕГН-то. Прочете целия лист внимателно още веднъж. „Жизнеспособни сперматозоиди – 0".

Чии бяха, тогава, трите му красиви дъщери?

СГЛОБЯВАНE

- Искаш ли кафе? – погледна го тя над очилата за четене.

- Не, благодаря.

Завъртя се обратно напред към масата и намести очилата. Отново се разнесе чевръсто тракане на клавиши. Той продължи да вади плоскости от кашоните и да ги трупа на купчинки около себе си.

След малко пак го загледа над очилата. Той работеше бързо и сръчно. Вадеше винтчета от някакви пликчета, поставяше една плоскост върху друга, после я отместваше, сверяваше нещо с чертежа, и се пресягаше за друга плоскост. Въпреки бързината, не изглеждаше притеснен или припрян. Приятно ѝ беше да гледа премерените движения на сръчните му тънки пръсти. Той не я поглеждаше, дългата коса падаше над очите му, но явно не му пречеше.

Погледите им се засякоха случайно. Той се усмихна.

НЕОБИЧАЙНИ РЕШЕНИЯ

- Само изглежда объркано. Ще стане.

Тя също се усмихна. Имаше хубава усмивка, с цяло лице. Бръчиците край очите ѝ личаха.

- Не се съмнявам.

- Май се уплашихте да не ви съсипя хубавата библиотека.

- Ха-ха-ха! Не! Напротив, много сръчно работиш.

- Мерси. Не е сложно. Свикнал съм.

Тя стана от стола и тръгна към него. Беше дребна, с коремче и тънки глезени.

- Не стъпвайте тук боса, може да се убодете на нещо.

Тя спря, свали очилата от носа си и се почеса по главата.

- Мислех да ти помогна, ако искаш.

- Не, няма нужда. Нали ви казах – свикнал съм. Ако ми помагате, само ще ме забавите.

Тя го погледа известно време и каза:

- Все пак ще направя по едно кафе. Аз така и така ще пия.

- Добре, тогава.

Тя тръгна към кухнята и той я проследи с поглед. Като я гледа човек отзад, годините не ѝ личат толкова. Е, мекото поясче около талията издава нещо, но изглежда приятно. Червеникавата ѝ коса беше небрежно вдигната на тила с някакъв шарен ластик, от късите ръкави се подаваха приятно загорели ръце.

- Извинявай, че те зяпах така преди малко, но си много приятна гледка. Отдавна не бях виждала млад човек да работи така сръчно и компетентно. Вече свикнах да гледам младежта да виси по кафенетата, заета с нищонеправене.

- Е, аз не мога да си го позволя.

- Сигурно си женен?

- Не.

- Гадже?

Той замълча.

- Нещо такова.

- Симпатична дефиниция.

Той пак замълча.

- Извинявай, това са си лични работи. Аз съм една любопитна лелка.

- Не, няма проблем. Просто не съм наясно със себе си напоследък.

- Welcome to the club – английският беше изненада.

- Абе, предполага се, че на моите години вече трябва да съм наясно, но... – последните му думи се изгубиха във внезапния грохот на бормашината. Той не гледаше към нея. Беше заел неудобна поза, като с ляво коляно беше заклещил една от плоскостите да не мърда, докато с дясното притискаше друга към земята.

- Е, „твоите години“ позволяват все още неориентираност – тя седна на най-близката табуретка и подпря лакти на коленете си. С лявата ръка държеше чинийката, а с дясната чашката кафе. – Смяташ ли да учиш нещо или си харесваш занаята?

Той провери дали дупките съвпадат, постави винтче и натисна спусъка на машината. Когато воят заглъхна, тя продължи:

- Извинявай, пак почнах да те разпитвам. Извинявай. Правя го, без да искам.

- Не, няма проблем. Просто не мога да правя две неща едновременно – ако почна да ви отговарям, ще завия винта накриво.

Изправи се, изтупа колене и се пресегна за чашката.

- Благодаря за кафето. Всъщност съм последна година. Два пъти прекъсвах, че трябваше да поработя. Сам се издържам – каза го със стеснение.

- Поздравления! – в гласа ѝ имаше такова възхищение, че той я погледна с интерес. – Наистина, поздравявам те. Явно си някакъв представител на много рядка, изчезваща порода. Какво следваш?

- Вътрешна архитектура.

- Значи почти си работиш по специалността – засмя се тя.

- Да, опознавам професията отдолу нагоре. А занаята научих от татко.

- Но имаш и талант. Много си сръчен.

- Мерси. Стига това да беше комплимент – добави след кратка пауза.

- Комплимент е, разбира се! Ако имах дъщеря, направо те вземам за зет – тя отново се засмя с цяло лице и бръчиците около очите ѝ се очертаха ясно.

- Едва ли може да имате толкова голяма дъщеря – той се почувства длъжен да ѝ върне комплимента.

- Ама ти трупаш червени точки с шампионско темпо! И комплименти знаеш да правиш! Да не би случайно да си на 45, а годините да не ти личат?

- Сега вече наистина не знам дали това беше комплимент.

- От моите уста – да. Извинявай, но все по-трудно намирам представители на вашето поколение, с които да водя свестен разговор. И да, имам синове почти на твоята възраст.

- Не може да бъде! – този път изненадата му беше съвсем неподправена.

- Не може, но е факт – тя се изправи, взе чашките и ги занесе в кухнята. Като се върна, седна пак зад компютъра и сложи очилата. – Няма да ти преча, работи си.

- Как ми се иска и приятелката ми да разсъждаваше като вас! – той седеше на стола срещу нея и я гледаше над капака на отворения лаптоп. Пиеха втора чаша кафе.

- За кое?

- Тя се срамува от това, че работя занаятчийска работа и се издържам сам. Предпочита да не го споменавам в компания.

- Защо? – в гласа ѝ имаше истинска изненада.

- Защото техните са ѝ внушили, че не е много изискано да се работи. Просто трябва „да имаш пари“. Не, че са много богати, имат някакво магазинче за хранителни стоки в Чепеларе, но са я възпитавали като „гранд-дама“. Живее в луксозна гарсониера в Лозенец, ходи с Мини-купър на лекции, маникюр и педикюр всяка седмица... ей такива работи. Иначе е много умна, сладурана е, добра душица, но не можем да се разберем по въпроса за работата и парите.

- Тя какво следва?

- Психология.

- Тежка наука.

- Ами! Тя следва за престиж. Нали ви казах, много е умна и с лекота си взема изпитите, помни като дявол. Но изобщо не смята да работи. Развила си е някаква теория – как щяла да дава под наем имоти и да не работи никога. Постоянно ми опява, че затъпявам от бачкане.

- Тя затъпява – гласът ѝ беше рязък, а очите разширени от гняв. – Виж, не я познавам, но направо ти казвам – бягай от нея! Жена, която по цял ден мисли за маникюри и солариуми е най-лошият възможен партньор в живота. Завършен егоист. Нима искаш да живееш с егоист?

- Май съм готов да го преглътна.

- А децата ти?

Той я погледна с неудобство, сякаш беше надникнала в разхвърляната му стая.

- Рано е да мисля за това.

- Ясно... извинявай, пак ти се бъркам.

Тя вдигна очилата пред очите си и се върна към екрана. Той усети, че я е разочаровал, а кой знае защо не му се искаше. Странно, знаеше, че разочарова Рени (Хи-хи-хи, не даваше да й казва Райна. Стана му смешно, като се сети.), но това не го тревожеше особено, беше го приел като част от пейзажа. А виж, да разочарова тази непозната му се струваше непоносимо. Неудържимо искаше да й направи добро впечатление.

- Синовете ти с теб ли живеят? – попита след неловка пауза, неусетно преминавайки на „ти“.

- Не, в чужбина са. Учат и се издържат сами. Също като теб – гласът й беше сдържан, но все пак го погледна над очилата.

- Значи, живееш сама?

- Защо реши така?

- Ами... – сега вече наистина се смути и не знаеше какво да каже.

- Защото си викам майстор да ми сглоби библиотеката? Или защото такива любопитни лелки-многознайки няма кой да ги трае? – в гласа й имаше малко сарказъм, но вече звучеше със закачка. Той усети примирието.

- Моля ти се! Не съм го и помислял даже. Но библиотеката е аргумент, признай си – добави след къса пауза.

- Мъжът ми е фотограф и пътува. Иначе е доста по-сръчен от тебе и досега да е сглобил тая библиотека. Но това означаваше да прескачам кашоните още две седмици, докато се прибере. А аз работя вкъщи и щях да се изнервя. Така ще му направя изненада.

- Ясно. Е, имам да сглобя още една секция и съм готов. Мерси за кафето.

- Ако си гладен, мога да ти направя нещо.

- Не, благодаря – тя усети колебанието в гласа му.

- Спокойно, мога да готвя. Обичаш ли спагети?

- Всичко обичам.

- Хайде, ти довърши тук, а пък аз ще приготвя нещо за хапване. И аз съм гладна.

- Добре, благодаря – и той се върна към бормашината. Незнайно защо поканата ѝ го развълнува неимоверно, нямаше търпение да седне на една маса с нея. Обзе го предчувствие за някакво важно преживяване.

- Извинявай, защо реагира така преди малко?

- За кое?

- Когато говорехме за приятелката ми.

- Забрави, не е моя работа.

- Не, интересно ми е.

- Остави, не трябваше да се паля. Не ме засяга. Просто имам синове почти колкото теб и се мъча да разбера мисленето ви.

- Толкова ли е важно всичко да е перфектно?

- Моля?

- Перфектно. Ти май искаш всичко да е перфектно. Дори да не те засяга.

Тя се засмя кратко и остави вилицата.

- Да не би психологията да е заразна? Всъщност, знаеш ли...
– тя положи ръцете си до лактите от двете страни на чинията.
– Нищо не е по-далеч от истината! Аз съм възможно най-несъвършеният човек на света. Имам един куп недостатъци, част от които продължавам да осъзнавам.

- Например? – гласът му беше тих и внимателен.

- Например, изпускам момента – тя поклати глава и отново се зае със спагетите. – Не оценявам колко важно е това, което имам в момента. Постоянно чакам нещо хубаво, страхувам се от нещо лошо, мисля за утре, за другото лято, за старостта... – гледаше замислено пред чинията си и въртеше спагетите на вилицата. – А важното е човек да усети мига, да го преживее, да го погълне и съхрани завинаги.

Той се хранеше много тихо, уплашен, че някой внезапен звук ще прекъсне потока.

- Веднъж бях на Халкидики. На един огромен пуст плаж. И в продължение на половин час изживях пълнота. Не знам дали ме разбираш. Абсолютно задоволяване на всички сетива. Пълно блаженство – гласът ѝ замря, очите ѝ се затвориха, ръката продължаваше машинално да върти вилицата. Пръстите ѝ бяха фини, с издайнически кафяви петна тук-там.

- На теб случвало ли ти се е? – тя отвори внезапно очи и го погледна с любопитство. – Така, да изживееш момент, в който си казваш: „Сега, тук, в този момент аз изпитвам пълно блаженство“?

- Май не. Или ако ми се е случвало, съм пропуснал да го регистрирам.

- Ето, това е проблемът. Изпускаме. Това е един от най-големите ми недостатъци. Изпускам. И после съжалявам. Но този момент не го изпуснах. Поне него.

- Опиши ми го.

Очакваше някакво смущение, отдръпване, затваряне в черупката. Така постъпваха повечето жени, с които беше общувал. Притесняваха се за своята перфектност. Смятаха, че ги харесва с ореоли. Но тя го погледна само с любопитство.

- Наистина ли ти е интересно? Това са си мои глупости.

- Да, много. Честна дума. Напоследък и аз си мисля за тези неща. Май имам същия недостатък.

- Добре – тя остави пак вилицата, сложи лакти на масата и се наведе напред. – Това е съзнателно, целенасочено регистриране на усещания. Просто си лежах там на пясъка, усещах топлината на слънцето, бриза по кожата си. Усещах как вятърът обръща косъмчетата по ръцете ми, как ми гъделичка ушите и си казвах: „Това е пълното сетивно блаженство“. Гледах слънцето и облаците, сиво-бялата светлина върху морската вода, една двойка гларуси, които летяха в съвършен синхрон, все едно някой ги движи с общо въженце; гледах как морето живее, мърда, диша, движи се и се питах: „Има ли по-красива гледка от тази?“ И си отговарях: „Няма. Значи, това е пълното зрително блаженство“. Слушах плясъка на морето, далечната музика и търкането на камъчетата при отдръпването на вълните – шум, който мога да слушам вечно. Слухово блаженство. И накрая вдишах с пълни гърди аромата. Любимия ми аромат – море, вятър, хвойна, билки, напечени от слънцето камъни. Нещо такова... – завърши тя и се върна към спагетите.

Той искаше да преглътне, но не можеше. Имаше чувството, че ако преглътне, ще избухне в плач. С цялата си душа пожела да живее с тази жена до края на живота си. И изпита буквална физическа болка от мисълта, че това няма да се случи. Тя шумно смукна последната спагета и облиза устни.

- Май не ти хареса моето готвене?

- Не, не... – той се стресна. – Просто се бях замислил.

Тя беше стара, за Бога! Можеше да му е майка. Почти. Шията ѝ беше поувехнала, а корените на косата ѝ – бели. Когато се движеше с гръб към него, виждаше разширените капиляри около глезените ѝ. Не изглеждаше зле с дрехи, но... Всъщност, и тя имаше маникюр! Сега забеляза. Погледна краката ѝ. И педикюр! Просто не говореше за тях! Имаше други теми за разговор.

- Сигурно ти прозвуча откачено. Но аз предпочитам да не пропускам тези неща. Животът е прекалено кратък. Ето, на мен ми е останало по-малко, отколкото съм преживяла досега. Влязла съм във втори сезон. И съжалявам за пропуснатите хубави серии от първи сезон.

- Не се ли притесняваш какво ще си помисля за теб, като говориш така?

Тя се засмя отново с хубавия си смях.

- Отдавна спрях да се притеснявам какво ще си помислят хората за мен. Но ми отне доста време и болка да осъзная, че е правилно. Затова реагирах така на мерaците на приятелката ти за безгрижен паразитен живот, в който най-голямата тревога е да не ти се счупи маникюрът. Аз самата имах такъв период и виж, от него се срамувам. Срамувам се какво е причинил моят егоизъм на мъжа ми и синовете ми. Слава Богу, осъзнах се навреме, за да не бъдат щетите фатални.

Тя отнесе чиниите до мивката. Започна да реже плодове и да слага парченцата в блендера, полуобърната с гръб към него.

- Обичаш ли ягоди?

- Обичам.

- Всъщност, знаеш ли кое е най-важното от всички чувства? – замълча и той се зачуди какъв отговор очаква.

- Любовта?

- Любовта днес е прекалено размито и комерсиализирано понятие. Всеки хормонален порив се брои за любов. Не ме карай сега да ти чета трактати за любовта.

- Тогава кое?

- Благодарността! Най-важното от всичко е да бъдеш благодарен! Благодарност е равно на щастие!

Тя пусна копчето и изчака блендера да смели плодовете. Извади две големи чаши и разпредели течността. Побутна едната към него.

- Да си благодарен означава да осъзнаваш какво имаш. Да мислиш за него, а не за това, което нямаш. Да си благодарен означава да изпитваш хубави чувства към хората. Да си благодарен означава да изживяваш пълноценно ето такива мигове. Ето, сега аз съм благодарна. Много.

- На кого?

- Първо на теб – за това, че ми сглоби така хубаво библиотеката; за това, че си толкова приятен и възпитан човек. Защото можеше да си някой шумен простак, който да ми одими целия апартамент с цигарите си. И да ми подхвърля цинични забележки. А ето, ти си толкова мил, умен и приятен младеж.

Той буквално се изчерви.

- Хубава работа! Бива ли да благодариш за такива неща!

- Бива, естествено. Второ, благодарна съм на Бог, че изпрати теб, че имахме такъв интересен разговор, че ми хареса спагетите. Оценявам този момент и го прибирам в сейфа с хубавите преживявания.

- Май аз трябва да ти благодаря – гласът му беше тих, погледът забит в масата.

- Добре, хубаво е да си бъдем благодарни един на друг.

Всъщност – мислеше си той, докато шофираше в следобедния трафик – Бог си знае работата. Ако тази жена можеше да ми роди деца и ако беше свободна... Рени просто няма шанс.

Телефонът му иззвъня.

- Кажи, коте.

- Нали не си забравил за довечера?

- Не съм, коте.

- И моля ти се, кажи че идваш от фитнес или нещо друго. Не споменавай гадната си работа. Не искам да мислят, че съм си хванала гадже от село.

- Аз няма да дойда, коте.

- Защо?

- Защото не мога.

- Но ти обеща! – гласът отсреща качи една октава.

- Знам, съжалявам. Но имам още един обект и ще съм каталясал. Няма да съм добра компания. И престани да наричаш работата ми „гадна“.

- Ох, омръзна ми! Вече се чудя какво да измислям, за да оправдавам отсъствията ти!

- Ами, престани да се чудиш. Просто кажи, че гаджето ти е сериозен мъж и работи, за да се издържа сам, а не чака на мама и тате.

- Ох, невъзможен си!

- Да, чао – и затвори.

ЗАДРЪСТВАНE

Наистина последен шанс. Друг няма да има.

Толкова лъжи, толкова разочарования, толкова натрупано недоверие... Този път обещанието трябва да се спази. „Ще бъда при теб в десет“ – така ѝ обеща и ще бъде, пък после да става каквото ще.

Тръгна рано, да избегне утринното задръстване. В седем часа вече беше на магистралата. Слънцето се издигна над планината и му светна право в очите.

Така ли щеше да е? Цял живот? Напрежението някъде между стомаха и диафрагмата не изчезна нито за миг през тези шестнайсет месеца. Знаеше какво иска; знаеше, че иска нея; знаеше, че и тя го иска. Но нито за секунда напрежението не изчезна. Страх. Че няма да разбере навреме желанието ѝ; че тя няма да приеме шегата му; че ще закъснее за среща; че ще я свари в непредвидено настроение; че ще се появят неканени хора; че тя ще му се стори неприятна и вулгарна; че той ще ѝ се стори неприятен и вулгарен...

Не си го представяше така. Очакваше някакво безметежно спокойствие и разбиране с погледи; постоянен смях и гъдел; лудешки кикот и бързи прошки; и най-вече – никакво напрежение. Мисълта за такова напрежение до края на живота беше като трън под нокътя. Но въпреки това не искаше да я изгуби. Не си представяше никакъв сценарий за раздяла.

Снощи пак. Дълги хленчещи обвинения по телефона. Повтарящи се обяснения; унизителни извинения. Обеща, че ще дойде и докато не изяснят всичко, няма да си отива.
- Няма да дойдеш, знам. Пак ще се обадиш в „без десет“, за да ми кажеш, че имаш важен ангажимент.
- Ще дойда. Нямам по-важен ангажимент от теб.
- Дано си сигурен. Защото нали знаеш... доверието ми в теб изтъня до косъмче. Още една пързалка няма да понеса. Ще бъде последна.

Как успяваше винаги да го постави в поза партер? Защо все той се извиняваше и обещаваше? Пак това гадно напрежение.

- Нали ти обещах? Ако не дойда, тогава мрънкай.

- Не, няма да мрънкам. Просто ще изчезна от живота ти. Ама наистина.

- Недей така. Дай да не се изнервяме сега по телефона. Утре ще говорим спокойно, очи в очи. Чакай ме в десет.

Дали да ѝ се обади, да ѝ каже, че е тръгнал вече? Не, ще я събуди. Сигурно спи още. Пък и няма какво да се отчита като ученик. Направо пристига точно в десет и толкова. Мъжка дума.

Като мина тунела при Траянови врата, увеличи скоростта. Спусна се към долината, а слънцето вече беше достатъчно високо, за да го скрие със сенника. Погледна часовника – осем без петнайсет. Като нищо щеше да е в Пловдив преди девет. Даже щеше да има време да изпие едно кафе и да си подреди защитната реч. Пусна разсеяно радиото. Напрежението почна да се разсейва.

Какво пък... най-лошото, което може да се случи, е да се разделят. Не, едва ли ще се стигне дотам. Все пак не са тийнове на по шестнайсет. Ще се разберат като големи хора.

На няколко километра след отклонението за Пазарджик стоповете на колите пред него внезапно светнаха. Стресна се и скочи на спирачката. Разтревожено погледна в огледалото, слава Богу следващата кола беше на достатъчно разстояние. За малко да удари червеното рено пред себе си! Двете ленти се изпълниха с коли за секунди. След малко потеглиха на пресекулки. Опита се да види какво става, не можа. Пет метра, стоп... десет метра, стоп... три метра, стоп... Очакваше да види катастрофа или нещо подобно след малко, но нямаше. Половин час... четиресет минути... добре че тръгна по-рано!

По едно време му се стори, че в съседната лента опашката върви малко по-бързо. Изчака един шофьор в нея да се заблее и сръчно се вмъкна пред него. Сега пък другата лента тръгна по-бързо! Няколко пъти се задминаваха с едно сиво комби, пълно с надути пояси отзад. Постепенно комбито набра преднина и се изгуби напред. А той се беше натресъл зад автобус, който бълваше дизелови газове. Затвори прозорците и пусна климатика, но миризмата пак влизаше. Отляво постепенно го настигна ван с немска регистрация, пълен със забрадени жени. Полека-лека и той го изпревари. По едно време между двете ленти мина мотоциклетист, завидя му искрено. През няколко минути по някой хитрец даваше газ отдясно и поемаше по аварийната лента. А нали в такива ситуации тя беше запазена за линейки и полицейски коли. Но на хитреците не им пукаше. Започна да ги псува наум.

С тревога следеше часовника на таблото, надигаше се да види какво става отпред, сменяше станциите на радиото с надежда някъде да съобщят нещо. В десет без двайсет дори не беше близо до Пловдив. Разбра, че ще трябва да ѝ се обади. Опашката отпред мръдна, но дребната микра отляво не. Задмина я и видя на волана момиче с големи очила, което притеснено въртеше ключа. Беше изгаснала и не можеше да запали. След малко неговата лента отново спря, той погледна в огледалото. Още стоеше там, не помръдваше, а зад нея изнервените шофьори свиреха. Дожаля му, пусна аварийните, слезе и притича назад.

- Проблем?

Момичето притеснено го погледна.

- Загря и я изгасих, а сега не ще да запали.

- Освободете скоростния лост, ще ви бутна. Слезте, ако искате, аз да опитам.

Тя не възрази, слезе припряно. Той се вмъкна бързо и завъртя ключа. Аха, беше я задавила. Завъртя няколко пъти за кратко, без да подава газ. Запали. Вдигна поглед и видя усмивка на облекчение върху лицето ѝ.

- Много ви благодаря!

- Няма проблем. Не я гасете повече и не я форсирайте. Нека акумулаторът да зареди.

- Добре, благодаря.

Слезе и отново се затича към своята кола. Чак сега видя, че си е захвърлил телефона на съседната седалка. Четири неприети повиквания. Напрежението го връхлетя с нова сила. Погледна часовника – десет и петнайсет. Обзе го някакво чувство на обреченост. Ами, това беше. Явно не им е било писано. За секунда го обзе раздразнение срещу очилатото момиче с микрата. Ако не беше загаснала така... какво ако не беше загаснала? Щеше да се измъкне от задръстването и да стигне навреме?... Е, поне щеше да звънне навреме... и какво, ако беше звъннал навреме? Щеше да звънне, само за да съобщи, че не може да си спази мъжката дума... Добре де, той какво е виновен, че има задръстване. Да не е с хеликоптер?

Набра номера с усещането за поражение.

- Ало?

- Няма нужда. Не си прави труда. Вдигнах, само за да ти кажа, че няма нужда да се разкарваш до Пловдив.

- Чуй ме...

- Сигурна бях, че ще стане така. И знаеш ли, дори не съм разочарована.

- Недей така, в задръстване съм.

- Не ти се сърдя, но не идвай. Няма да съм си вкъщи. Изтрий номера ми от телефона си.

- Защо не искаш да ме изслушаш?

Тишината му подсказа, че е затворила. Набра я отново. „В момента няма връзка с този номер.“ Раздразнение, обида, надигащ се гняв... и някаква съвсем микроскопична капчица усещане за свобода. Удовлетворение, че филмът е завършил точно както е предвиждал.

Бибиткането отзад го стресна. Смрадливият дизел се беше придвижил сто метра напред, а той все така стоеше с телефона в ръка. Даде газ. Изравни се с микрата. Махна на очилатката вътре и свали прозореца.
- Всичко наред ли е?
- Да, много ви благодаря!
- Лек път!

Още малко се придвижваха така на прибежки по стотина метра и ту тя минаваше пред него, ту той пред нея. Някъде напред видя мигащи светлини и разместване в плътните гирлянди от автомобили. Явно наближаваха причината за задръстването, каквато и да беше тя. Но вече нямаше за къде да бърза. И в Пловдив нямаше за какво да ходи. На първата отбивка ще обърне обратно за София. Но преди това ще спре на някоя бензиностанция. Двете кафета и двете минерални води от сутринта досега напираха да излязат. А и беше гладен.

Най-сетне! Напряко на две от лентите се беше проснал в цял ръст бял хладилен камион. Полегнал на една страна като повален слон-албинос, с неприлично щръкнали колела и безсрамно извадени на показ вътрешности. Около него разтревожено щъкаха полицаи и разни хора с телефони. Не видя линейка и това малко го успокои. Сигурно шофьорът е заспал... или е спукал гума, кой го знае. Сигурно беше един от щъкащите. В аварийната лента имаше две полицейски коли, вероятно чакаха кран или нещо подобно да отмести трупа на камиона.

След това движението изведнъж се отприщи. Изнервените от чакането в жегата шофьори нервно натискаха газта и всеки гледаше да се шмугне пред другите. Вдясно се очерта силуетът на бензиностанция. Да, няма за къде да бърза.

Подаде десен мигач и отби. Явно не беше единственият, чиито естествени нужди бяха изострени от задръстването. Пред тоалетната имаше опашка. Запъти се към ресторанта в дъното на паркинга с надежда неговата тоалетна да е по-достъпна. Микрата седеше спретнато и кротко между два ТИРА-а. Затъмнените ѝ стъкла проблясваха. Дали е същата? Не помнеше номера. Но цветът съвпадаше.

Сблъскаха се на входа. Тя излизаше със сандвич и кафе в двете ръце и се опитваше да си отвори с крак. Той пък имаше само една цел – тоалетната. За малко да ѝ разсипе кафето.
- Извинете! – вдигна извинително ръце.
- Няма нищо, не успяхте да го разсипете.

Погледите им се срещнаха и двамата се засмяха смутено. Очите ѝ проблясваха сребристи зад очилата.

- Вие ли сте! Радвам се, че ви видях. Не успях да ви благодаря както трябва. Много ме е срам за изгасването.

- Моля ви се! На всеки се случва.

- Не, настоявам да ви купя поне едно кафе.

Последното, от което имаше нужда сега, беше кафе.

- Не, няма нужда, наистина. Благодаря. Приятно и безаварийно пътуване!

- Тогава поне сандвич.

- Не, недейте.

Тя усети, че се мъчи да я разкара.

- Вие бързате сигурно. Извинявайте – усмихна се смутено и разочаровано.

- Не, просто трябва да ида до тоалетната – сега той се смути.

- Боже, съжалявам! Колко съм недосетлива! Добре, ще ви изчакам.

Понечи да каже „няма нужда", но усети, че ще е невъзпитано.

- Извинявайте, идвам след минута.

Минутите станаха повече от пет, защото и пред тази тоалетна имаше опашка. Дори си помисли, че няма да я завари. Но тя седеше на една от масите отвън, отпиваше кафе и гледаше разсеяно паркинга.

- Извинете, че се забавих, имаше опашка.
- Няма нищо. Не бързам за никъде.
- Не може да бъде. Всеки бърза за някъде.
- Не и аз. Докато висяхме в задръстването, разбрах че вече няма смисъл да бързам.
- И аз! – засмя се на глас.

Един ТИР точно пред тях запали и двамата подскочиха.
- Ке бегаме или ке се биеме?

Тя се разсмя с цяло лице и цяло гърло.
- По-добре да бегаме, че съм си забравила пушката.

Преместиха се на друга маса, той също си купи сандвич и кафе. Очакваше всеки момент напрежението да поникне някъде там, на обичайното си място – между стомаха и диафрагмата.

Не поникна. Тя се смееше много заразително.

НЕОБИКНОВЕНО РЕШЕНИЕ

В автобуса имаше места, но тя умишлено не седна. Никога не сядаше. Особено зимата. Ледените седалки от напукана изкуствена кожа пробутваха студа си през вълнената пола и бедрата ѝ се замразяваха трайно. Полата беше вълнена, но разкроена и отдолу постоянно подвяваше студ. И все пак, като стоеше права, с крака плътно долепени един в друг, тя усещаше поне част от собствената си топлина.

Пазеше равновесие в средата на „колелото", подпряла гръб в отвесната тръба и дишаше повърхностно през зъби, за да усеща колкото може по-слабо дизеловото зловоние, изпълнило раздрънкания Икарус. Вратът ѝ беше вдървен от напрежение и студ, гледаше втренчено през мръсните прозорци. Улиците бяха съвсем тъмни, още се влачеха най-кратките дни от годината. От време на време пробягваха улични лампи с влажни оранжеви ореоли. По друсането и залитането знаеше кога наближава нейната спирка. Придвижи се към вратата с походката на моряк върху палуба в бурно море.

Вратите се отвориха със съскане и тя стъпи право в ледена каша от вода и сняг. Автобусът бе спрял твърде далеч от бордюра и тя не успя да скочи. Усети лявата си ботинка пълна с лед. Добре че живееше на десет минути от спирката. Започна да подтичва, за да се стопли, но беше прекалено хлъзгаво, залитна няколко пъти и реши да не рискува.

Първото, което направи, като се прибра, беше да се преобуе. С топлите чорапи и пантофи постепенно започна отново да си усеща краката. Прибра синята престилка в стаята си, свали бялата якичка, изпра я на ръка над мивката в кухнята и я простря на сушилника над печката. Изпра си и чорапогащника, който беше мокър, дори кален. Така и ръцете ѝ се стоплиха. Отвори печката, не беше загаснала. Добави две дървета и доволно се усмихна. Сега щеше да стане истински топло.

На мивката намери тенджера с кисела зелка и върху нея бележка от майка ѝ: „Направи кисело зеле с ориз“. Зарадва се. Не само щяха да ядат зеле с ориз, което обожаваше, ами и майка ѝ беше извадила зелката от кацата, и сега тя нямаше нужда да бърка в ледената саламура! Наряза зелката и я сложи да ври.

Извади учебниците и тетрадките от чантата, провери си програмата за утре и притича до стаята си, за да смени едните учебници с други. Там беше ледено студено; влизаше в нея единствено за да спи. Както и в цялата къща, с изключение на кухнята, впрочем. Само там гореше стара тежка печка и беше топло. И там живееха. Тя, брат ѝ, майка ѝ и баща ѝ. Добре че през по-голямата част от деня бяха навън, та не стояха всички заедно в нея дълго време. Събираха се горе-долу само за вечеря. Затова тя бързаше да си напише домашните върху кухненската маса, преди да са пристигнали останалите.

Майка ѝ беше детски лекар и даваше дежурства на смени. Днес щеше да се прибере с последния автобус в десет часа. Баща ѝ свиреше в оркестъра на операта и тази вечер имаха представление. Щеше да се върне към полунощ, обикновено го докарваше някой колега с кола. Брат ѝ беше втора смяна на училище и щеше да си дойде след около час. Дотогава тя трябваше да е приключила с домашните и уроците.

Нищо сложно. Колко лесен и приятен щеше да е животът, ако най-големият ѝ проблем бяха уроците! Както беше за останалите ѝ съученици. Те се притесняваха единствено дали няма да ги изпитат по химия, дали ще имат контролно по математика и как ще си напишат темите по литература. За нея това бяха смешни неща. Истинската тежест в гърдите ѝ идваше от другаде.

Понякога си мислеше дали Господ не се е подиграл с нея. Не беше възможно на едно осемнайсетгодишно момиче да се струпат всички гадости, които двадесети век може да измисли. Да се родиш не просто в малка комунистическа страна, ами и в протестантско семейство! Две взаимно изключващи се вселени. И на всичкото отгоре, в беднотия.

Че комунизмът е нещо лошо, научи лично от баща си още преди да произнесе правилно думата „комунизъм". В същото време ѝ беше обяснено, че ако тя дори само веднъж, дори съвсем случайно и макар с най-добри намерения се изпусне пред когото и да било, че той е казал такова нещо, ще има баща в затвора. Още не знаеше да чете, но вече знаеше как да води двойнствен живот. В училище учеше стихотворения за партията, участваше в рецитали и дори минаваше за примерно пионерче, а вкъщи слушаше „Свободна Европа" заедно с баща си и автоматично затваряше прозорците, когато го видеше, че пуска ВЕФ-а на 13 метра къси вълни.

Внимаваше никой в училище да не научи, че тя ходи на църква. Това беше възможно най-гадното, което можеше да ѝ се случи. В часовете на класния им четяха лекции, че религията е опиум за народите и на църква ходят само простите бабички по селата. И тя се срамуваше, че е проста бабичка, която поема опиум. В същото време обичаше да ходи на църква, там имаше приятелки, нямаше нужда да води двойнствен живот и всички бяха много задружни. Тормоза, на който бяха подложени, полулегалните събития, които организираха, ги обединяваха. Тя обожаваше да ходи на планински екскурзии с приятелите си от църквата, да катери чукари, да седи вечер край огъня, да тананика заедно с останалите, да флиртува невинно с момчетата.

Само родителите ѝ да не бяха толкова консервативни! Майка ѝ имаше склонност към аскетизъм. Да правиш нещо за удоволствие беше грях. Ако някаква дейност нямаше поне малко практично полезно приложение, се считаше за неуместна. Ако една дреха имаше някакви други функции, освен да покрива тялото и да топли, се считаше за неуместна. Ако една храна служеше за нещо друго, освен да достави енергия на тялото, също се считаше за неуместна. Затова и готвеше почти без подправки, със съвсем малко мазнина и много рядко блудкави воднисти десерти.

А Нина беше различна! Имаше трапчинки на двете бузи и обичаше да се смее. Обичаше да яде вкусни неща, да облича красиви дрехи и да изпитва удоволствие. Но дяволската комбинация, в която се беше родила, категорично ѝ отказваше всичко това. Вкусните неща изобщо не влизаха в семейното меню (освен ако не са полезни!), а храненето навън беше напълно непозната дейност. Беше скъпо, имаше прекалено малко заведения и в тях предлагаха „вредни“ неща. Нина сама се научи да готви, като четеше готварски книги, както се четат романи – с настървение и упоение. Представяше си вкуса на ястията само по описанието на съставките. Но дори и готвенето беше голямо предизвикателство, просто защото трудно можеше да намери всички необходими продукти. От кварталната бакалия купуваха каквото има в момента и каквото са „пуснали“. И въпреки това скоро започна да готви по-вкусно от майка си. Майка ѝ мърмореше, че манджите на Нина са прекалено мазни и с много подправки, но тя получи неочаквана подкрепа от баща си, който щедро я хвалеше. И майка ѝ бързо ѝ преотстъпи пространството около мивката, защото така или иначе не обичаше да готви.

За красиви дрехи и дума не можеше да става. На училище ходеха с униформа, а родителите ѝ ясно заявиха, че нямат пари за „двойни“ тоалети – тоест за униформени и за такива, които се носят извън училище. А в нейната гимназия беше въпрос на чест и престиж, ако те видят из града в неучебно време, да си „издокаран“. Е, Нина нямаше как да е издокарана. И в неучебно време си ходеше с бели блузи и черни поли, най-много връзваше по някое цветно шалче да не ѝ се подиграват, че и извън училище ходи с униформа. Нови обувки се купуваха, когато старите се скъсат.

Освен това „издокарването“ беше в противоречие със суровата пуританска религия на семейството ѝ. Всякакви неща, свързани със „светската суета“, се считаха за ужасен грях. Така Нина не просто беше в графата „селска бабичка, пушеща опиум“, ами и принадлежеше към едно религиозно малцинство, считано дори от традиционните попове за фанатично и вредно.

За нея беше цяло чудо, че имаше приятелки. Е, не бяха кой знае какви приятелки – нито една от тях не я считаше за „най-добра“ приятелка, беше на второ-трето място в списъка на всяка от тях, но поне не беше сама и изолирана. Имаше с кого да се мотае из междучасията и да ходи на кино тайно от майка си. (Защото и киното спадаше към излишните удоволствия.) Но и приятелките си задържаше с помощта на доста лъжи. Криеше, измисляше си, фантазираше... Живееше в един почти измислен свят, който представяше пред другите за чиста истина. Рядко я хващаха в лъжа и почти винаги успяваше да се измъкне с разни обяснения.

Освен това беше адски добра ученичка и всички преписваха от нея домашни, контролни, есета, реферати. По време на класно пишеше не само своето есе, но поне на още двама.

НЕОБИЧАЙНИ РЕШЕНИЯ

Никога не искаше нищо в замяна и може би затова част от съучениците ѝ се чувстваха длъжни да се отплатят най-малкото с добро отношение.

Беше красива. Макар изобщо да не смяташе така. За нея, както и за почти всички в тази възраст, „красив“ означаваше „добре облечен“. А тя беше грозно облечена. Затова спортната ѝ фигура, класически черти и прекрасни очи не впечатляваха никого. Включително и самата нея. Завиждаше на съученичките си, които получаваха любовни бележки от момчетата, но не защото харесваше тези момчета, а заради вниманието, което момичетата получаваха. Когато получи първата любовна бележка, се почувства развълнувана и поласкана, макар изобщо да не харесваше момчето, което я пращаше.

Този двойнствен живот я напрягаше ужасно и изпълваше с неудовлетворено раздразнение. От време на време в домове на съученички и приятелки разглеждаше Некерман или Бурда и не можеше да повярва какви красиви дрехи съществуват на този свят. Гледа филма „Роки“ поне десет пъти. Не защото харесваше бокс или спортни филми! Не, пази Боже! А просто защото обичаше кадрите, в които Роки тича в утринния здрач между небостъргачите на фона на музика. Какви красиви градове има по света! Обичаше да гледа и френски, и италиански филми, просто защото в тях се виждаха улици, кафенета, магазини и къщи от един друг свят. Онзи, за който баща ѝ казваше, че е истинският, а те живеят в кошмар. Най-много обичаше да гледа комедиите на Луию дьо Фюнес — защото бяха смешни, защото там караха красиви коли, бяха облечени с модерни дрехи и живееха в хубави къщи.

Баща ѝ имаше колеги, емигрирали на Запад, от които научаваше това-онова. Дори от време на време носеше вкъщи по някой шоколад, донесен „отвън“. Нина и брат ѝ си го деляха до последната трохичка и го ядяха като Свето причастие.

Докато решаваше бързо уравненията по органична химия, които имаха за домашно, тя не спираше да мисли. Но не можеше да го измисли. Предстояха ѝ три неприятни неща и тя се чудеше дали може да ги избегне, кои от тях и евентуално как. Сякаш три гадни железни тежести бяха притиснали стомаха ѝ.

Първо, трябваше по някакъв начин да съобщи на техните, че в училище им събират пари за новогодишното празненство. Всяка година имаше разправии по този въпрос. „Няма да ходиш на разни глупави празненства!“ — отсичаше обикновено майка ѝ. Но Нина настояваше, че е задължително, иначе ще им пишат отсъствия. Не, не беше задължително, но за нея беше. И без това постоянно отсъстваше от всякакви събирания с дрескод „издокаран“, защото нямаше какво да облече. Сега празненството щеше да е след часовете, така че всички щяха да са с униформи. И на нея ужасно ѝ се искаше този път да е като другите, да не ѝ се налага да измисля разни тъпи извинения, а да празнува с останалите.

„Само знаят да искат пари! – мърмореше баща ѝ. – Кажи им, че нямаме.“ Ето, това нямаше да им каже дори ако трябва да си отхапе езика. Комунизъм, не комунизъм – в нейната елитна гимназия беше срамно да си беден и да казваш, че нямаш пари. А и тя доста си беше съчинявала и фантазирала за задграничните командировки на баща си и въображаемите си роднини в чужбина. „Не може. Всички ще дадат“ – отговаряше винаги. Накрая, естествено, ѝ даваха, но подчертаваха, че това означава зачеркване на новогодишния подарък. Тя се съгласяваше. Макар че после ѝ се налагаше да съчинява пред съучениците си какви подаръци е получила. Сега ѝ предстоеше същата битка, дори може би още по-лоша, защото вчера брат ѝ беше поискал пари за същото и беше получил след голяма разправия. Страхуваше се, че ще си го изкарат на нея и ще компенсират похарченото за брат ѝ, като спестят от нея.

Второто неприятно нещо беше предстоящата „битка“ с учителя по история. Беше скучен и посредствен историк, който си зубреше и каканижеше уроците от учебника, но беше партиен секретар и следователно, важна клечка в училището. Беше научил, че тя ходи на църква и родителите ѝ са религиозни. Извика я на личен разговор в кабинета си, попита я дали е вярно и буквално ѝ нареди да престане да ходи на църква, и да напише декларация, в която заявява, че не споделя възгледите на родителите си. „Иначе се прости с мечтата за университети, ясно ли е?" – излая срещу нея, надвесен над бюрото си. Точно зад главата му имаше портрет на Карл Маркс и брадата му стърчеше от двете страни на даскала като козина на колобус. На Нина ѝ стана смешно, но я беше прекалено страх, за да се засмее. Излезе, без да каже нищо.

Докато се прибираше, мислеше какво да направи. Да предаде родителите се, не можеше. Да заяви, че не вярва в Бог също не можеше. Защото вярваше. Може би малко му се сърдеше и не го разбираше, но вярваше. Струваше ѝ се съвсем естествено да вярва. Глупостите, които учеха в часовете по биология – за произход от амеби, чехълчета, зелени еуглени, ихтиозаври, плезиозаври и разни „-питеци" – ѝ се струваха абсолютно смехотворни. Трябваше ѝ много повече вяра, за да повярва в тях, отколкото в логичната идея за Разум, който е създал и поддържа всичко.

А Нина беше честен човек. Въпреки лъжите и фантасмагориите, в които се заплиташе, докато омайваше съучениците си, тя беше честна пред себе си и пред родителите си. Не, не можеше да ги предаде. Но какво ще каже утре на гадния дебел историк? И по-важно – как щеше да реагира той? Дали щеше да я изложи публично пред всички? Дали щеше да направи така, че да я изхвърлят от гимназията? Дали щеше да ѝ превърне живота в ад? Страхуваше се.

И третото неприятно нещо, което ѝ тежеше, беше, че идва Нова година. По принцип, Нова година е хубаво нещо. Ваканция, празници, подаръци, трапези... Но тя не искаше Нова година да идва. Гърлото ѝ беше сгърчено от тежко оловно предчувствие, че в момента изтича най-хубавата, последната хубава година от живота ѝ, а Нина не искаше тя да свърши. През новата я очакваше може би изключване от училище. Може би унижения пред всички. Но най-вече в старата година оставаше най-прекрасното изживяване, което няма как да се повтори. И докато годината все още не беше изтекла, тя го усещаше като свое настояще. Влезеха ли в новата, то щеше да бъде вече минало.

През лятото на тази година тя се влюби. Нямаше никаква надежда, разбира се. Между нея и него стояха твърде много неща, твърде много години, хора и предразсъдъци. Но все пак тя му беше благодарна за усещанията, които я накара да изпита. Никой никога досега не беше ѝ казвал, че е красива.

Не беше ѝ го казвал истински. С очи, пълни с възхищение. „Не мърдай, много си красива така." И тя наистина не мръдна, защото не повярва на ушите си – за пръв път в живота ѝ някой ѝ затвори устата. А той сръчно развъртя обектива на фотоапарата си и завъртя друг, по-дълъг. След това се отмести заднишком, както си седеше в тревата, и започна да фокусира. Тя понечи да се облегне на другата ръка, че тази ѝ беше изтръпнала. „Не мърдай!" – долетя отново до нея. Тя застина, вперила смутен поглед в изпъкналото око на обектива. „Сега си завърти главата наляво и погледни към стената!" Тя изпълни нареждането вдървено. „Точно така! Не мърдай!" Тя не смееше да мръдне, макар ръката ѝ съвсем да изтръпна. Почувства някаква странна топлина, като си помисли, че през издутото око на обектива той я гледа и я харесва.

Емил не беше като глупавите ѝ съученици. Беше истински мъж. И то добър мъж. И я гледаше с мъжко възхищение. Много ѝ се искаше да я целуне, но не знаеше как ще реагира, ако той наистина го направи. Той не го направи. Дори не се опита. Държеше се джентълменски, говореше ѝ за фотография, обясняваше ѝ за цветовете в светлинния спектър, караше я да му говори на английски, на френски, на руски и все се смееше. Не, не ѝ се присмиваше, а искрено се смееше от радост и гордост, че я познава. Повтаряше ѝ, че е направо удивително красива и тя изчервена приемаше комплимента, без да му вярва. Само се чудеше защо ѝ го казва.

След месец той ѝ изпрати дебел плик със снимки. На всички беше тя. Прекрасни изискани черно-бели снимки, на които тя приличаше на онези френски актриси, които гледаше на екрана. Като ги видя, майка ѝ вдигна страшен скандал, скъса няколко, но Нина се разплака, хвърли се срещу нея, изтръгна ги от ръцете ѝ и избяга в стаята си. После скри останалите под двойното дъно на ученическата си чанта, под всички учебници. И всеки ден по няколко пъти проверяваше дали са там и дали не са се смачкали. Майка ѝ поиска обяснение, обвини я, че се е държала неморално, заплаши я и поиска да знае какъв е този развратен фотограф. Отказа да ѝ повярва, че между Нина и него не е имало абсолютно нищо и насила я заведе на гинеколог, за да се увери, че дъщеря ѝ е все още девствена.

Нина писа на Емил дълго благодарствено писмо, няколко пъти го къса и преписва. Ту ѝ се струваше, че звучи прекалено фамилиарно и лигаво, ту пък, че е прекалено официална и студена. Наистина не знаеше как се пишат писма на мъж. Ана Каренина и Наташа Ростова не можеха да ѝ помогнат. Прекалено отдавна бяха живели, прекалено различни бяха любовните им истории. Не посмя да му напише за реакцията на майка си, нито да признае, че няколко снимки бяха унищожени. Емил ѝ отговори почти веднага, в писмото имаше още снимки. Този път Нина има късмет да прибере пощата преди майка си и скри писмото. Цяла седмица се чуди дали да пише на Емил. Страхуваше се, че ако завържат постоянна кореспонденция, рано или късно ще трябва да го изправи срещу майка си. Още повече се страхуваше, че ако спре да му пише, той ще я забрави.

Накрая реши да си постави знак – ако той ѝ пише още веднъж, без тя да му е отговорила, значи наистина я харесва и няма да се откаже от нея. Тогава ще му отговори, пък каквото ще да става. Той не ѝ писа.

След няколко дни последният лист от календара с грозен пейзаж и цифрата 1988 във всеки от четирите ъгъла, щеше да бъде откъснат и на негово място тържествено да бъде закачен новият с още по-грозен пейзаж, на който пишеше 1989. Нина гледаше двете осмици и очите ѝ заплуваха в сълзи. Никога, никога повече магията на осмиците нямаше да се върне! Следващият път, когато на календара ще има две осмици една до друга, ще бъде през 2088 година! Когато нея отдавна няма да я има!

Какво ли имаше да стане през тези сто години? Дали наистина комунизмът щеше да изчезне, както злорадо коментираше баща ѝ? Той беше толкова щастлив, когато през тази година разрешиха пътуванията в чужбина! Беше един от първите, които седяха две нощи на опашка, за да се сдобият с червен паспорт! Така влюбено го разглеждаше! И не спираше да говори за колегата си от Виенската филхармония, който му уреждал документите да отиде там. Нина го слушаше и не й се вярваше. Даже се страхуваше. Дали пък баща й няма да замине и повече да не се върне? Или пък ще ги вземе със себе си? Не смееше да го попита.

Дали тя щеше да стане актриса, както си мечтаеше? Дали щеше да се омъжи за Емил и да има деца? Какви ли деца щеше да има? И дали щеше да е възможно с него да отидат да живеят в Нова Зеландия, примерно? Или някъде също толкова достатъчно далече, че да не могат да се върнат, и да забравят всичко тук?

Дали щяха да се появят летящи автомобили? Дали парите щяха да изчезнат? Дали хората щяха да се превърнат в риби? В ума й се залутаха всякакви фантасмагории от книги, които беше чела, и се оплетоха. Очите й продължаваха да се взират в осмиците, но сълзите й пресъхнаха. Кое точно ще има значение след сто години? Дали ще има правнуци? Как ли ще се казват? Къде ли ще живеят? Дали държавата й ще съществува и дали изобщо ще съществуват държави? Дали пък светът няма да е свършил и земята да е необитаема? Интересни или страшни неща ни очакват?

Нина чу пътната врата да се отваря и разбра, че брат й се прибира. Обзе я внезапно чувство, че сега, веднага, в този момент трябва да вземе някакво много съдбоносно решение. Сега, през тези няколко секунди, преди той да е влязъл. Какво точно? Не знаеше. Но знаеше, че то ще определи всички нейни решения до края на живота ѝ.

- Избирам, избирам... да вярвам! – каза изведнъж на глас и в този миг брат ѝ отвори вратата на кухнята.

- Какво? – избоботи той, свали изпотените си очила и започна да ги бърше.

- Нищо. Здрасти.

- Здрасти. Какво ще ядем за вечеря? Кисело зеле?

- Кисело зеле.

- Какво каза, като влязох?

- Нищо. Уча едно стихотворение наизуст.

- Виж това – и извади от чантата си нещо увито във вестник. Махна вестника и тържествено разгъна пред Нина червена тениска, на която с бели букви пишеше ПЕРЕСТРОЙКА. Обърна я като фокусник. На гърба ѝ пишеше ГЛАСНОСТЬ.

- Откъде я взе?

- Купих си я.

- Не може да ходиш с нея на училище.

- Може. Съветска е.

- Не може, ще видиш.

- Ти ще видиш какво има да става.

- Какво?

- Догодина по това време пак ще си говорим.

- Стига дрънка глупости, иди да донесеш дърва от бараката, че сложих последните.

- Помни ми думата! – извиси глас брат ѝ, докато излизаше – Догодина по това време комунизмът ще е паднал!

Нина се засмя и отиде да добави ориз към зелето. Провери за всеки случай дали брат ѝ е излязъл и отново повтори на глас: „Да, избирам да вярвам!“ И се засмя. Защо и тя не знаеше. После сложи чайника на печката, за да има гореща вода за грейките, когато тръгнат да си лягат. Във всички стаи беше по-студено, отколкото в хладилника. Мъничките горещи грейки бяха като горещи сърца в ледените чаршафи – единствен източник на радост и топлина.

Нина прибра учебниците в чантата си, закачи бялата якичка на престилката си, погледна отново двете осмици на календара и установи, че железните тежести в стомаха ги няма. Може би не тази година, може би дори не и след десет години, но тя щеше да бъде това, което иска. Щеше да бъде обичана такава, каквато е. И около нея щеше да бъде светло и топло. На всички.

В този миг токът спря. Нина с автоматичен жест се протегна за кибрита и запали свещ.

ПРОДЪЛЖЕНИЕ

Първото професионално ориентиране получи от баща си:

\- И най-забутаното село има нужда от три неща – кръчмар, бръснар и гробар. Тези тримата никога няма да умрат от глад. От мен да го знаеш.

Само че неговите амбиции се простираха далеч отвъд „да не умре от глад". Десет години търка банките в университета. Не защото беше слаб студент, не! Напротив, беше отличник и взимаше стипендия. Но за две магистратури и един докторат отиват тъкмо десет. И по чужбина беше, обиколи три европейски университета по програмата Еразъм, говореше свободно два езика, освен английския. На всичкото отгоре, беше само сантиметър под един и деветдесет, атлетичен, носеше косата си по-дълга от обикновеното и се гордееше с нея.

НЕОБИЧАЙНИ РЕШЕНИЯ

На трийсет смяташе, че светът е почти в краката му.

Почти. Докато спечели Маги. След това вече светът наистина беше в краката му.

Извади чашите от миялната. После започна внимателно да ги реди на рафта. Провери колко мляко е останало в хладилника и пусна кафе-машината да загрява. Първите клиенти щяха да дойдат всеки момент.

Не стана нито гробар, нито бръснар, а кръчмар. По-точно, кафеджия.

Разочарованията започнаха в мига, в който се изкачи на върха на света.

Първо, удари на камък с работата. Трябваха му две години, за да осъзнае тъжния факт, че темата на дисертацията му вълнува цифром и словом нула човеци по белия свят. Постепенно започна да снижава критериите, беше готов да работи дори като учител в гимназия. И работи пет години. Достатъчно, за да разбере, че е несъвместимо със запазването на здрав разсъдък.

Разочарованията на личния фронт се развиха някак успоредно. Кривата на любовта се плъзна надолу. Искаше му се Маги да беше останала мечта. Материализирането на мечтата угаси светлината ѝ. Най-големият удар нанесе новината, че тя не може да има деца. Маги се затвори в себе си и се обиди на целия свят – на Господ, че е постъпил така несправедливо с нея; на него – че иска дете; на родителите си – че не са открили навреме заболяването ѝ; на лекарите – че са толкова безпомощни; на приятелките си – че забременяват и раждат без проблем.

Борис с изненада установи, че всъщност, винаги е искал да стане баща, да има свое продължение, да рита футбол със сина си, да гледа на кръв първите ухажори на дъщеря си.

Тягостният период съвпадна с отрезвяването на професионалния фронт и горчивото осъзнаване, че докторатите и магистратурите му могат спокойно да отидат в едно и също кошче с бащинството. Започна да се чувства като неудачник. Логичният ден на раздялата с Маги дойде естествено. Имаше твърдо намерение да започне отначало още веднъж. Но не се получи.

На трийсет и пет години направи най-откаченото нещо – стана донор на сперма. След една дълга нощ на тихо самотно пиене и един ден на горчиво изтрезняване реши, че не иска семката му да се изгуби. Сякаш беше нещо много ценно. Пожела някъде някое негово дете да се появи като огромен късмет в живота на самотно и отчаяно семейство. Неговата семчица да замести безплодната семка на някой обезверен мъж. Почувства се като глухарче, на което вятърът отнася семенцата и то никога повече не ги вижда. Но продължава да съществува в тях.

Разрови в интернет и разбра какво трябва да направи. Много бързо го одобриха. За пръв и последен път дипломите и езиците му направиха огромно впечатление и той веднага беше „поканен“ за донор. Когато го попитаха има ли някакви белези и особености по рождение, отговори отрицателно и вътрешно се подсмихна. Нямаше как да разберат, защото още на двайсет си оперира невъзможно клепналото ухо. Точно заради него започна да носи дълга коса още като ученик. И когато събра достатъчно пари и смелост, отиде да му го оправят. Повечето му познати дори не знаеха, че по рождение едното му ухо беше като на катерица, а другото идеално залепнало за главата. Стори му се забавно вълнуващо някой ден да види на улицата детенце с едно залепнало и едно щръкнало ушенце.

После... после завоят беше плавен, сякаш беше стигнал предела на разочарованията и спря да се разочарова от каквото и да било. На четиресет и пет си спомни за гробаря, бръснаря и кръчмаря на баща си и отвори кафене, каквото нямаше в радиус от три квартала. Редовни клиенти му станаха банковите служители от четирите банки наоколо, както и повечето чужденци от голямата офис сграда отсреща. Именно заради езиците. Беше им приятно да разменят по някоя дума на своите езици с изтънчения мъж зад бара – винаги облечен изискано, с културен глас и запас от пикантни вицове. Борис намери някаква радост и утеха в общуването с хората, опозна толкова съдби, научи такива невероятни истории, че сериозно се замисли да напише книга. Вечер се веселеше дискретно, запазваше пълна анонимност на гостенките си и затова рядко му отказваха. Беше почти щастлив.

Към три следобед беше мъртво време. Отбиваха се само случайни.

- Добър ден – вдигна глава от книгата и погледна кой е.

- Добър ден, заповядайте.

Тринайсет-четиринайсетгодишен пубер с напъпили мустаци и рошава глава. Такива рядко влизаха. Този, обаче, беше възпитан. Каза „добър ден“. Повъртя се в средата и накрая се паркира на масата до прозореца. Отиде при него, усмихна му се и го попита свойски:

- Искате ли нещо? – винаги говореше на Вие, дори на тригодишните.

- Ъъ, има ли уай-фай?

Усмихна се и посочи стикера на витрината:

- Естествено. А ще пиете ли нещо?

- Една ко́ла.

Тръгна към бара да вземе ко́лата, хлапето се провикна след него:

- И едни фъстъци, ако може.

- Разбира се.

Докато сипваше фъстъците в купичка, огледа хлапето. Дълго, кльощаво, несъразмерно, напомни му за него самия като малък. Внезапно хлапето се облегна назад и се почеса по врата. С опакото на ръката си! Едва не изтърва подноса. За пръв път виждаше някой да се почесва така. Освен себе си. Беше страшно неудобно и неефикасно. Изобщо не облекчаваше сърбежа. Но от малък го правеше, без да знае защо. И естествено, не беше виждал да го прави никой друг.

Седеше зад бара и чак се изпоти от напрежение, докато се мъчеше да измисли нещо. Накрая го измисли. Докато разчистваше масата в ъгъла, една празна кутия от фанта излетя „случайно“ и падна на пода до хлапето. То се стресна и вдигна очи.

- Извинявайте! – гласът на Борис беше пълен с разкаяние. – Ужасно съжалявам! Удари ли ви?

- Не, не – малкият се засмя и личицето му стана съвсем детско. После се наведе да вдигне кутията.

Наблюдаваше го втренчено. При движението косата му падна напред и оголи щръкнало ушенце. Като на катерица.

БИНОКЪЛ

Аман от котки!...

Подритна мазната опаковка, пъхна плика подмишница, бръкна в джоба за ключовете, изтърва си телефона и изруга. Естествено, падна върху мазната опаковка. Вдигна го гнусливо с два пръста и тръгна по стълбите. Качването на стълби е здравословно. Особено след трийсетте.

Особено след трийсетте... от днес. Гадост. Отключи, влезе и мазният телефон звънна. Ха сега де! Пусна всички чанти и пликове, влезе припряно в банята, откъсна тоалетна хартия и почна да го трие. Без да иска, затвори. Нищо, поне ще го изтрие като хората. Порови в шкафа в банята, сипа дезинфектант върху ново парче хартия и изтри старателно дисплея. Той пак звънна. Непознат номер.

- Ало?

НЕОБИЧАЙНИ РЕШЕНИЯ

- Имате пратка. Може ли да слезете долу?

- Кой е?

- Куриер – гласът бе равнодушен и изпълнен с досада.

Да не би някой да се е сетил за рождения му ден?... Да, естествено. Баща му. Милият пазач. Охранител. Бивш старшина от запаса. Пенсиониран преждевременно, щастлив, че може да охранява единствената банка и единствения банкомат в градчето. Много обичаше да го поучава и назидава. Сигурно е книга. Или нещо друго „полезно".

Заключи, седна на дивана и разкъса куриерската опаковка. Хм, тежко е.

„Скъпи сине, навлизаш в най-продуктивната възраст за един мъж. Гордея се с теб. Надявам се вече да помислиш и за други житейски решения, освен кариерата си. След 18 месеца договорът ми изтича, ще имам повече време и ще мога да се отдам пълноценно на внуче.

Честит рожден ден!"

Надписът беше на ръка, със стегнатия дисциплиниран почерк на баща му. Картичката стандартна, с букет отпред и червен надпис „Честит рожден ден". Вероятно, единствената възможна опция в пощенския клон на града. Стана му смешно за „другите житейски решения".

Бинокъл! Баща му беше изпратил бинокъл! Рефлекторен, марков, водонепроницаем. Кой знае колко струваше. „Татко съвсем се е смахнал! Какво да правя с бинокъл в София? Да ходя на лов в Южния парк? Или да следя катаджиите отдалеч?“

Повъртя го, изчете приложението с инструкциите, впечатли се, погледна през него. Какво да гледа? Стената е на четири метра. Забележителен фокус, нощно виждане.

Излезе на терасата, подпря се на парапета и го насочи към далечината. Опа... не очакваше такова ясно приближение. На светлината на залязващото слънце изведнъж видя черупки от гълъбови яйца по керемидите на отсрещната съборетина. Уау! Дори пукнатините по керемидите се виждаха! Започна да движи бинокъла бавно и да се наслаждава на гледката. Все едно се беше покатерил на покрива. Продължи надолу. Олук, задно дворче с каменни плочи и трева между тях, платнен шезлонг със захвърлено върху него одеяло и книга... завъртя фокуса и прочете: „Мадоната с коженото палто“.

Мазилката беше стара, но двата прозореца отпред – нови, дори лепенките на фирмата производител още стояха по дограмата. Защо си бяха хвърлили парите? Най-късно до една година тази съборетина ще отлети като къщичката на Дороти и на нейно място ще изникне новичка кооперация с малки балкончета, гаражи и миниатюрна тревна площ отзад. И тогава ще може да надрича през прозорците на хората с бинокъла...

Тази мисъл го развесели. Като по филмите... тайно ще наблюдава паралелния живот на столичани. Усърдни трудещи се през деня, примерни граждани, които си плащат ипотеките... и се отдават на фантазиите си, щом се затворят между четирите стени на собствения дом.

Яркосиньо. Усети, че от няколко секунди наблюдава нещо яркосиньо. Тишъртката на момичето в двора с шезлонга. Мъкнеше двукрака стълба. Подпря я на керемидите и почна да се катери по нея. Стана му интересно и увеличи зума. Виждаше съсредоточената ѝ физиономия с прехапано езиче. Ръцете ѝ бяха бели, без следа от солариум. Тишъртката ѝ беше широка, през изрязаните ръкави се виждаше розов сутиен. Стана му неудобно. Къде се беше закатерила така? Погледна по-нагоре и видя котенце, сгушено на втория ред керемиди. Пак котки!

Момичето стигна ръба на покрива и се протегна. Не стигна до котенцето. Качи още едно стъпало и пак се протегна. Котенцето се премести на третия ред керемиди. Момичето погледна към краката си, постоя нерешително за миг и после внимателно се качи на последното стъпало. „Опасно е, бе момиче! Виж я само... детска работа! Ще се пребие заради едно коте!“

Момичето полетя назад заедно със стълбата. Той подскочи, извика, бинокълът падна от очите му. Добре че беше каишката. Припряно го вдигна пак и трескаво фокусира. Котенцето бавно слизаше към съседната ограда. Потърси момичето. То лежеше неподвижно на плочките, стълбата – върху него, а шезлонгът беше паднал на една страна. „Мадоната с коженото палто" не се виждаше никъде.

Той се изправи уплашено, понечи да извика, но усети, че ще прозвучи глупаво. Без бинокъл гледката беше неясна и далечна. Падналото на земята момиче приличаше на захвърлеп работнически гащеризон. Той погледна нагоре, настрани, надолу... никой, освен него не беше видял. Не се колеба повече.

Хвърли бинокъла на дивана, пъхна телефона в джоба си, грабна едно шише вода от хладилника и хукна.

Момичето беше в безсъзнание, виждаше се и кръв, но не можеше да разбере откъде точно. Беше дребничка, пухкава, с красив бюст под тишъртката. Но сега устните ѝ бяха гадно лилави. Той трескаво набра 112, хвана китката на момичето и усети пулс.

Да я премести? Не, в интернет беше чел, че пострадалите не бива да се местят, за да не се увредят допълнително. Боже, дано да дойдат по-бързо! Дойдоха.

Пое ангажимент да заключи къщата и да намери данните ѝ.

****

НЕОБИЧАЙНИ РЕШЕНИЯ

До осем часа имаше време. Мивката беше пълна с чинии, килимът трябваше да се постеле след тупането, оставаха и шест въпроса от конспекта, но човек трябва и да си почива, все пак! Добре че поне Центърът по хемодиализа беше в съседната пресечка, та ѝ трябваха само пет минути. Сега ще дремне половин час, после ще измие чиниите, ще постеле килима и ще вечеря. Като включи първите пациенти към апаратите, ще има половин час да прехвърли поне един въпрос от конспекта. После, като се прибере към дванайсет, ще мине и останалите. Ще останат поне три часа за сън. Супер.

Не, това не се траеше! Някой трябва да забрани на тези котки да се котят постоянно и навсякъде! Мяучеше някъде точно над главата ѝ. Тъничко, плачливо, но постоянно. Направо китайско мъчение! Стана, нахлузи тишъртката, излезе и заобиколи зад къщата. Измъкна старата стълба на хазяйката и я помъкна по посока на мяученето. Дали е стабилна? Разтърси я с ръка, изглеждаше стабилна. Тръгна бавно нагоре. Уф, че мразеше високото!

Аха, ето го престъпникът! Ела тук, мац, писи, писи... настръхнало, черно-жълто, с ококорени сини очи, котето мяукаше на равни интервали като навита играчка. Протегна се. Не става. Добре, има още едно стъпало. Пак се протегна. Докосна пуха, но котето се уплаши и се дръпна назад. „Да ти се не види! Ще се пребия заради теб!“ Погледна надолу, плочките изглеждаха доста далеч. Мамка му, ако го остави тук, ще мяучи поне три дни! Ох, я да се хване с едната ръка за олука. Изглежда здрав.

****

Старшината в оставка, пенсионер и охранител на единствената банка и единствения банкомат в града Красимир Стратев направи доволен оглед на апартамента. Ходеше бавно, с отмерена войнишка крачка, скръстил ръце зад гърба, като отваряше и затваряше вратите, сякаш пропускаше гости. Навсякъде беше безукорно чисто, миришеше на ароматизатор. Отвори гардероба. Критичният оглед не откри нередности и там. Мина в кухнята. Преброи бутилките в хладилника, премести салфетника от шкафа върху масата, избърса невидими трохи от нея, поклати се доволно на пръсти и пети.

Видя сивата кола да паркира долу, мина в коридора, огледа се в огледалото, приглади косата над лявото ухо с привичен жест, премести снимката на жена си един сантиметър наляво върху шкафчето с обувките и с искрици в очите зачака звънеца.

- Значи, чудо – казвате? – старшина Стратев се беше облегнал назад на дивана, преметнал крак връз крак, прострял лявата си ръка върху облегалката.

- Ами, няма друго обяснение – смутолеви Сими. – Такова немислимо стечение на обстоятелствата... как да го наречем по друг начин?

- Ти сега добре ли си? Няма да има някакви трайни последици, нали?

- Казаха, че няма. Е, гърбът ме боли като стоя права, лявата ръка не мога да я вдигам колкото дясната, но сякаш друго няма.

- А главата? Как не си я ударила?

- Явно съм паднала върху книгата.

- Излиза, че четенето на книги е животоспасяващо! – засмя се Димо. – Пък били те и кримки на Агата Кристи.

- Каква Агата Кристи?

- „Мадоната с нещо си“... Да не би да е Реймънд Чандлър? Не знаех, че има такава книга.

- Али Сабахатин – каза Сими с подигравка в очите.

- Кой?

- Али Сабахатин. Авторът на „Мадоната с коженото палто“.

- Това псевдоним ли е?

- Не.

- Турчин да пише за мадони?

- Не се смей, ами я прочети. Много хубава книга.

- Да не би някоя мадона да е попаднала в харема на султана?

Старшина Стратев се наведе енергично напред и доля чашите.

- Наздраве за чудото!

- Наздраве за твоя бинокъл, татко! Все едно някой ти е подсказал да ми го изпратиш! Не ми каза колко си се изръсил за него.

- Наистина ми подсказаха.

Димо погледна баща си с любопитство. Сими също. Но той не каза нищо, само отпи с маниер.

Дори пижамите на старшина Стратев бяха безупречно изгладени с ръбове. Той се придвижи тържествено от спалнята до хола, почука и като чу „да“, влезе, протегнал напред лявата си длан. Сими и Димо го погледнаха едновременно.

- Това са нашите халки с майка ти. Навремето ги купих от един тираджия. Малко се демоде, но вие дайте да ви ги направят както искате.

- Ама, татко! Ние имаме пари, няма нужда!

- Не съм казал, че имате нужда. Това е семейно злато – Димо го досмеша на тържествения тон.

- Добре, татко, много ти благодарим.

- Лека нощ.

- Лека нощ – отговориха двамата едновременно.

Сгушени на дивана Сими и Димо разглеждаха дебелите златни халки. Димо го обхвана някаква нежна тъга. Спомни си ръцете на майка си – с дълги пръсти, малки нокътчета и фини руси косъмчета по китките. Миришеха на крем за ръце, когато го завиваха вечер. Отвън на липата се беше покатерила котка, а отдолу два котарака ѝ правеха серенада.
Аман от котки!

Старшина Стратев затвори Евангелието, свали очилата, сложи ги внимателно върху шкафчето, целуна снимката на жена си, сключи ръце за молитва и тихо произнесе: „А когато беше още далеч, баща му го видя... Боже, благодаря ти, че ми подсказа за бинокъла. Никога нямаше да се сетя". После легна на една страна и заспа веднага, по войнишки.
Отвън серенадата продължаваше.

ТЕРАПИЯ ЗА СЪРЦЕ

по истински случай
1957

„Научете се да приемате смъртта, колега. Пациентите ни не са безсмъртни. Не може да спасите всички.“

Тези ужасни думи кънтят в ушите му, докато държи ръката ѝ и малката ѝ глава като на лястовичка потрепва върху възглавницата. Диша на пресекулки, но не спира да му разказва за какво мечтае – да се научи да играе сложното Еленино хоро, да роди момчета-близнаци и да пее с пълно гърло по време на морска буря от върха на нос Калиакра.

„Сепсис...“ Смъртна присъда, която ще бъде изпълнена до края на седмицата. Какво да прави, освен да я обича до края? Ще престане да бъде лекар и ще бъде само мъж. Ще свири

„елениното“ на устна хармоника и ще подскача смешно около леглото ѝ, за да я разсмива... ще падне на коляно и ще я помоли да му окаже честта да стане баща на близнаците ѝ... ще ѝ обещае да крещи заедно с нея от върха на Калиакра.

Възрастните професори ще клатят глави със съчувствие и насмешка едновременно и великодушно ще го освободят от задълженията му, докато всичко свърши. Нищо не може да спаси инфектираното ѝ сърце. Нека поне да бъде щастливо, когато спре да бие...

2007

Дамян и Сава се споглеждат и едновременно забавят крачка. От доста години вече единият живее в Германия, а другият в Америка; единият говори с жена си на немски, а другият на английски. Но свръхестествената им способност да мислят в синхрон не е изчезнала. Връзката, изплетена още в майчината утроба, с лекота ще преодолява всякакви разстояния, докато са живи.

Оставят майка си – мъничка, цялата в черно – да крачи напред сама. И двамата са усетили, че тя иска да остане насаме с баща им за последен път. Прочутият кардиолог д-р Ставрев не успя да спаси собственото си сърце. Но Бог беше милостив към него и децата му – държа го жив, докато те долетят от различните краища на света, за да си поговорят с него за последно.

- Не искам никакви погребения – шепнеше пресипнало той с посинели устни, полуседнал в леглото. – Ще ме кремирате и после само тримата ще занесете урната ми в гробницата. И после, като му дойде времето, ще сложите майка си до мен.

Не е честно да умре човек в началото на лятото, когато животът зеленее и се размножава с буйна сила. Майка им върви под сянката на огромните брястове по алеята на гробището и сама носи красивата урна с праха на баща им. Не им разреши да ѝ помагат.

- Дължа му го – каза им простичко тя. - Искам да усеща любовта ми.

И плътно обгърна с длани студения метал, за да го стопли.

Много пъти са слушали историята. Баща им я разказваше, майка им я разказваше, колегите на баща им я разказваха... историята за едно безнадеждно болно сърце, което било излекувано само с любов. Всеки си имаше своя версия. Те обичаха най-много версията на майка си – „Не посмях да умра – завършваше винаги тя – горкият, нямаше да му издържи сърцето“.

Тримата застават в мълчание. Майка им – дребничка, със зачервени и замечтани очи – в средата. И те двамата – като копия един на друг – от двете ѝ страни. Взират се в надписа върху урната, който майка им е поръчала да издълбаят: „Сърцето се лекува с любов. На моя любим кардиолог. Мира.“

После си тръгват и оставят д-р Ставрев насаме с шума на брястовете.